"This is not the *little* party you promised," Elizabeth cried. "Steven didn't say we could have a party in his apartment at all!"

"What do you want me to do about it?" Jessica asked her twin, her hands on her hips. "Tell people to stop having so much fun?"

"Well, for one, you can turn down the stereo and start telling people to find another party somewhere else," Elizabeth said. Just then she saw one of the Thetas step on top of the coffee table and start spinning and dancing to the music.

"She can't dance on there!" Elizabeth fumed. "Jess! Go tell your friend to get off the table right now!"

Jessica turned around to see what had got her sister so upset. But instead of urging the girl off the table, Jessica ran right over and jumped up next to her. The two girls started bumping their hips, bending their knees to dip lower and lower.

"You go girl!" another Theta called, clapping her hands to the beat. A number of other kids who had been talking or snacking jumped into the dance area. Someone turned up the volume on the stereo.

Elizabeth stood breathless as she watched the party becoming more and more chaotic. If Jessica wasn't going to help her, she would have to take control herself.

COLLEGE WEEKEND

Written by
Kate William

Created by
FRANCINE PASCAL

BANTAM BOOKS
NEW YORK • TORONTO • LONDON • SYDNEY • AUCKLAND

RL 6, age 12 and up

COLLEGE WEEKEND

A Bantam Book / October 1995

Sweet Valley High® is a registered trademark of Francine Pascal
Conceived by Francine Pascal
Produced by Daniel Weiss Associates, Inc.
33 West 17th Street
New York, NY 10011
Cover art by Bruce Emmett

ISBN: 0-553-56636-9

Published simultaneously in the United States and Canada

Bantam Books are published by Bantam Books, a division of Bantam Doubleday Dell Publishing Group, Inc. Its trademark, consisting of the words "Bantam Books" and the portrayal of a rooster, is Registered in U.S. Patent and Trademark Office and in other countries. Marca Registrada. Bantam Books, 1540 Broadway, New York, New York 10036.

PRINTED IN THE UNITED STATES OF AMERICA

OPM 0 9 8 7 6 5 4 3 2 1

To Alice Elizabeth Wenk

Chapter 1

Sixteen-year-old Elizabeth Wakefield scrutinized her outfit in the bathroom mirror. *Do I look too young in this?* she wondered as she straightened her yellow-and-white flowered T-shirt. *Maybe I should change.*

Elizabeth usually didn't worry about what she was wearing, but today was different. Today Elizabeth and her twin sister, Jessica, were leaving for a week-long visit to Sweet Valley University. They were planning to stay with their older brother, Steven, and his girlfriend, Billie, who were both students at the university.

Elizabeth had been on the campus of SVU only a few times—to drop Steven off or pick him up. Sitting in the backseat of the family car, she had gazed longingly out the window at the beautiful, tree-lined campus. As she had watched the students lounging on the grassy fields, or walking among the buildings with their arms laden with books, Elizabeth had fantasized about being a student. This week was her chance to make that fantasy come true.

Maybe I should wear something more mature, Elizabeth thought. *Something that would make people take me seriously as a college student, instead of Steven Wakefield's kid sister from high school.* But then Elizabeth remembered that she wanted to be taken seriously for her intellect, not for her clothing choices. She checked her reflection again in the full-length mirror on the back of the bathroom door. Her glossy blond hair was pulled back in a neat ponytail, and she was wearing crisp Levi's and clean white Top-siders. *You look fine,* she told herself. *Leave it to Jessica to make the fashion statements.*

Elizabeth suddenly realized that she hadn't heard a peep out of her twin all morning. Jessica's bedroom was on the other side of the bathroom they shared. *Maybe Jess slept through her alarm again*, Elizabeth thought.

She knocked on the door leading to Jessica's room. "Jess! Are you awake?" she called out.

"I'm awake," Jessica grunted from behind the door, sounding as if she was buried under three layers of blankets.

"Well, hurry up," Elizabeth said cheerily. "We want to get on the road by nine."

Jessica's only response was a low groan. Elizabeth smiled. Nothing was going to squash her excitement today, not even her sister's usual morning laziness.

Elizabeth picked up her toothbrush, which was the last item she needed to pack, and walked through her bedroom into the hallway to find her suitcase. She was surprised to discover that it wasn't at the top of the stairs where she had left it the night before after packing.

Elizabeth knocked on Jessica's door. "Jess! Are you sure you're up?"

The door opened. Jessica stood rumpled in her bathrobe. "I'm up, I'm up," she said, rubbing her eyes. "I was just waiting until you were out of the bathroom."

"That's a first," Elizabeth said. "*You* waiting for *me* to come out of the bathroom."

Jessica covered her eyes with her hands. "Please," she groaned. "No sarcasm first thing in the morning."

"Anyway," Elizabeth continued, "I was just wondering if you'd seen my suitcase. I left it in the hallway before I went out with Todd last night." Todd Wilkins was Elizabeth's longtime steady boyfriend.

Jessica blinked. "Right. Well." She paused, raking her fingers through her slept-on hair. "I guess I forgot to tell you."

Elizabeth sighed. "*What* did you forget to tell me?"

"Well, when I saw your suitcase sitting out here, I noticed that it was barely full," Jessica began. "It's so much bigger than my teeny one, so I didn't think you'd mind if I used it," she concluded sweetly.

"You what?" Elizabeth cried, incredulous.

"Don't get all bent out of shape, Liz," Jessica said.

"I packed your stuff into one of my bags. Besides, it's not like you really needed a suitcase this big—you just packed a bunch of jeans, T-shirts, and sweaters, so it doesn't matter if they get wrinkled."

"And what do you need all that room for?" Elizabeth asked, crossing her arms over her chest.

"Well," Jessica explained, "since I'm planning to prerush Theta Alpha Theta, I had to bring my favorite outfits. I can't make my college debut in wrinkled silks and linens, can I?"

Elizabeth smiled and shook her head. Theta Alpha Theta was one of the most prestigious sororities at Sweet Valley University, and their mother, Alice Wakefield, had been president of the Thetas as a senior. Jessica had been bubbling about Theta all week, especially after Mrs. Wakefield had brought down her old Theta memorabilia from the attic.

Although Elizabeth didn't share Jessica's enthusiasm about being in a sorority, she knew how important it was to her sister. She decided to let this one go.

"Jess," Elizabeth sighed. "Please *ask* next time, OK?" It wasn't the first time Elizabeth had been confronted with the differences between herself and her twin. Even though Jessica and Elizabeth looked identical on the outside—from their blue-green eyes, to their long blond hair, to the matching dimple in their left cheeks—their personalities could not have been more different. Elizabeth, the more responsible twin, chose to wear comfortable and practical clothes rather than fashionable ones—she didn't structure her life around the sales at the mall. Jessica did. And while Elizabeth loved to have fun, she never put off doing homework before socializing. Jessica did.

The twins' extracurricular activities were polar opposites, too. Jessica spent every afternoon choreographing and practicing new cheers as the cocaptain of the cheerleading squad, whereas Elizabeth spent her afternoons writing the "Personal Profiles" column for the school newspaper, *The Oracle*. Elizabeth's greatest desire was to be a journalist. Jessica wanted to be an actress, a rock star, or some other sort of celebrity.

"So what did you do with my stuff?" Elizabeth asked now.

Jessica pulled her robe tight around her waist and surveyed her bedroom. "Where did I put that thing?" The room was in its typical disarray, with four large piles of clothing and a thin layer of socks and papers scattered on the floor.

Elizabeth waited patiently while Jessica kicked at the assorted debris. "Aha!" Jessica exclaimed suddenly, bending to pull at a handle sticking out from underneath one of the larger piles. "Here we go," she said, holding out a bright-blue duffel bag. "It's my favorite one." Stenciled on one of the panels were the words "Sweet Valley High Cheerleading Squad."

Elizabeth sighed and grabbed the duffel bag by the handles. "Gee, thanks. I've always wanted one of these," she said sarcastically.

"You can't keep this, you know," Jessica said. "I'm just letting you borrow it."

"And I'm grateful," Elizabeth said, laughing. Jessica never could figure out why Elizabeth wasn't dying to be a cheerleader. "Hurry up and get ready," she reminded Jessica again. "I think Mom's got breakfast waiting for us. We don't want to be late for our first day of college!"

"How do I look?" Jessica asked as she entered the kitchen. She turned around slowly to let her family appreciate her outfit: hip-hugging white denim jeans and a boat-neck black-and-white-striped top. Her hair was twisted into a sophisticated upsweep.

Ned Wakefield whistled. "I have the most beautiful daughters in the world," he said fondly. Jessica smiled, but she didn't really need her family to confirm what the mirror had already told her. She knew she looked good.

Then Jessica noticed the breakfast feast on the table. "Yum! Bacon!" she cried as she pulled out a chair and joined her sister and parents at the table. "You never make bacon on Saturdays," she told her mother, helping herself to four pieces. "What's the occasion?"

"I think this morning qualifies as an occasion," Mrs. Wakefield said, her eyes sparkling. "It's not every day my favorite daughters go off to college." She poured orange juice into Jessica's glass.

Jessica took a sip of the juice. "And fresh-squeezed

orange juice?" she asked, incredulous. "Mom, it's not like we're actually going away to college."

"But you will be soon," Mrs. Wakefield said, reaching across the table to stroke Elizabeth's cheek. Elizabeth took her mother's hand and smiled.

Jessica watched their display of affection. "I can't believe how sappy you guys are getting about a week-long stay with Billie and Steven," she said, rolling her eyes. She ripped off a chunk of her breakfast muffin and popped it into her mouth.

"Now, Jess, I hope you're not thinking of this as a vacation," Mr. Wakefield said. Jessica recognized the telltale lecture expression on his face, and she groaned inwardly. "Consider yourself lucky," Mr. Wakefield continued. "It was very kind of Steven and Billie to let the two of you stay in their apartment for a whole week."

"Did I hear you use the words 'kind' and 'Steven' in the same sentence?" Jessica asked with a laugh. Elizabeth kicked her under the table.

Mr. Wakefield gave Jessica a stern look. "Steven and Billie expect you to be good guests, so make sure you show respect for their apartment." Steven had met Billie when he had advertised for a new roommate. When it turned out that "Billie" was female, the two of them had decided to try being roommates anyway, but they soon fell in love, and a real romance had blossomed between them.

"I told Steven that if you cause any trouble, it's back to high school for the both of you," Mr. Wakefield warned, looking from one twin to the other. "I don't want to hear about any fights breaking out between you and your brother—"

"Oh, Dad," Jessica said with a sigh. "Please. We've grown up. We don't get into silly fights anymore." Jessica and Steven had often argued in the past—both of them were opinionated and stubborn. But since Steven had left for college, their clashes had become less frequent.

"Furthermore," Mr. Wakefield continued, as if Jessica hadn't said a word, "your mother and I didn't ask Steven to let the two of you stay with him just so you can goof off for a week in the middle of the semester." He began buttering a slice of toast as he spoke. "We thought it would be good for you to really try to get a taste of the college experience, so you can put all your worries about grades and SATs in perspective."

Elizabeth began, "I never want to hear—"

"—those three letters again," Jessica finished for her. The twins' eyes met, and they laughed.

But now that the subject of the Scholastic Aptitude Tests had been raised, Jessica didn't really feel like laughing—or eating bacon; she felt like throwing up. A few weeks before, Jessica and Elizabeth had been gearing up, in their own individual ways, for their first attempts at the SATs. Elizabeth had worried and stressed out over the tests, studying furiously. Jessica, on the other hand, couldn't understand what all the fuss was about and didn't study at all. She even went out to dinner with her boyfriend, Ken Matthews, the night before the test.

The real shocker came when they got their scores: Jessica had done tremendously well, and Elizabeth's scores were mediocre. Elizabeth had been devastated, seeing her college career and her future disintegrate before her eyes. Jessica's concern was different: She was accused of cheating.

Jessica was infuriated that no one believed she was smart enough to do well on the SATs. That is, no one but Elizabeth. Elizabeth became her sister's greatest champion and successfully defended Jessica in front of the school and the test officials. And after taking the test over again, their scores had reversed: Elizabeth had got stellar scores the second time around, while Jessica's had been just average.

"If I didn't think that test was meaningless before, I sure think it's meaningless now," Jessica pouted, poking at her bacon.

"Unfortunately," Elizabeth said, staring woefully into her coffee, "the college-entrance officials don't think it's meaningless."

Jessica suddenly pushed her chair away from the table with a loud scrape on the tile floor. "Well, we've got a car to load up," she said. "Let's get moving." She wasn't going to let thoughts of the SATs get in the way of what was really important: planning a week of college fun and parties. Without waiting for Elizabeth to follow, she charged up the stairs to get her suitcase. *Leave it to Elizabeth to get all worked up about applying to college on this morning of all mornings,* she thought. *She'd better lighten up soon—before she ruins the whole week!*

Elizabeth was draining the last of her coffee when she heard her sister shriek in pain from somewhere upstairs.

"Jess, are you OK?" Elizabeth called worriedly as she ran out of the kitchen.

Elizabeth found her sister standing on the top landing of the staircase, warily eyeing the flight of carpeted stairs that stretched down to the front entrance of the Wakefield house. Elizabeth's suitcase, now overstuffed to the bursting point, leaned against Jessica's leg. "I'm fine," Jessica muttered. She grabbed the suitcase by the handle and heaved. It barely budged.

Elizabeth walked to the front door, where she had left her duffel bag. She easily picked it up and slung it over her shoulder. "Now do you wish you had packed for a week instead of a month?" she called up to her sister.

"Don't act so self-righteous," Jessica said, giving the suitcase a quick kick. "Do you think you could get Dad to give me a hand here?"

"Sure, Jess," Elizabeth said, smiling.

But Mr. Wakefield was already walking into the hallway. "You packed it, you carry it—that's what I always say," he said with a grin. Elizabeth stifled a giggle.

"C'mon, Dad," Jessica pleaded. "If I try this alone, I'm bound to break my neck."

"Well, I wouldn't want to be blamed for that," Mr. Wakefield joked. He climbed the stairs two at a time and bent to pick up the suitcase. "Here, let me—" He yanked on the handle of the suitcase and grunted under its weight. "Is it something in the genes that makes women overpack?" he complained.

"What was that, Dad?" Elizabeth called up to her father. "Did I hear an obvious sexist comment cross your lips?"

"No, no, no," Mr. Wakefield protested. "I can see that my *other* daughter didn't overpack."

"I just wasn't sure what I would need," Jessica explained as she followed her father down the stairs. "I don't know what sorority girls are wearing these days."

After Mr. Wakefield had successfully maneuvered the suitcase down the stairs, he dropped it beside the front door with a thud. "Jessica," he said sternly, "I don't remember giving you permission to go to a sorority party."

"They might have an open house, to get to know the members," Jessica told her father. "It'll be during the day." When her father still looked suspicious, Jessica quickly added, "It won't be a *party* party, Dad."

Just then a car horn honked outside. Elizabeth turned and opened the front door. Todd's BMW was pulling up in front of the Wakefield house. "Todd!"

she called. Elizabeth jogged across the lawn as the car came to a stop.

Ken got out of the passenger seat. "Is your sister around?" he asked Elizabeth.

"Ken!" Jessica squealed from the house before Elizabeth could answer him. She ran over to her boyfriend. "What are you guys doing here?" she asked.

"We couldn't let you two go off to college without giving you a proper farewell," Ken said. He opened his arms and Jessica gave him a big hug.

Elizabeth watched them embrace. She liked the fact that her sister had been dating Ken. Jessica used to be known for dating a lot of guys—any cute guy she met, in fact. But she seemed to be happy with Ken, and Elizabeth was glad that her sister had finally "settled down." Jessica and Ken seemed destined for each other—not only did they look great together, with their blond hair and athletic builds, but Ken was Todd's best friend, so it seemed somehow fitting that Elizabeth's twin was dating him. It also seemed fitting to Elizabeth that Ken, the captain of the football team and its star quarterback, was dating Jessica, the cocaptain of the cheerleading squad.

"We brought you bon voyage gifts," Todd said. He turned around to retrieve something from the backseat of his BMW.

"Oh! I almost forgot!" Ken added, joining Todd at the open car door. Elizabeth's face lit up when she saw the boys emerge with two big blue sweatshirts and two red roses.

"This is to help you fit right in," Todd said as he held out the sweatshirt to Elizabeth. The words *"Sweet Valley University"* were printed in white block letters on its front. "And this is to help you remember to come back," he continued, handing Elizabeth the rose.

"Oh, Todd," Elizabeth said softly. "I'm going to wear this sweatshirt every day I'm gone. That way I'll feel like you're always right there next to me."

"I'm going to think about you the whole time," Todd said, pulling Elizabeth close for a kiss.

Meanwhile Jessica had taken her rose and whisked it behind one ear, flashing Ken a flirtatious smile. "How do I look?" she asked.

"Beautiful," murmured Ken. "I'm going to miss you, Jess," he whispered, kissing her gently on the neck.

Jessica pulled back from his embrace after a minute. "Thanks for the presents, Ken," she said, tossing her sweatshirt into the backseat of the open Jeep. "Now, could you give me a hand with my suitcase?"

"Sure thing," Ken agreed, following Jessica into the house.

Elizabeth giggled.

"What's so funny?" Todd asked.

"Nothing, really," Elizabeth replied, giving her boyfriend's arm an affectionate squeeze. "It's just a good thing that Ken's such a strong guy!"

Moments later the Jeep was loaded up and Jessica and Elizabeth were safely buckled in. Jessica turned to glance at her sister in the passenger seat. Elizabeth was staring into Todd's eyes lovingly.

"Hey, Liz," Jessica prodded. "Let's get this show on the road. You'll see Todd in a week." Jessica never could understand her sister's long-term attachment to Todd. Although she had to admit Todd was cute, Jessica considered him much too dull.

"I know," Elizabeth replied softly, never taking her eyes from Todd's. "We've been separated before, and I know I'll be fine, but . . ."

"Maybe you don't have to stay the full week?" Todd suggested hopefully.

Elizabeth's eyes lit up, but before she could respond, Jessica threw the Jeep into reverse. "See you in a week!" she said merrily, giving a quick wave as the car lurched out of the driveway.

"'Bye, Todd! 'Bye, Ken!" Elizabeth yelled out the window, waving her arm furiously until the twins' boyfriends were just two small specks on Calico Drive.

"Sweet Valley U, get ready for the Wakefield twins!" Jessica shouted as she pulled the car onto the open road.

Chapter 2

"Isn't this week going to be amazing? I can't believe Mom and Dad are letting us take time off from school to have a college vacation," Jessica exclaimed, fussing with the car stereo to find a song she liked. She had set the volume to an ear-shattering level, and Elizabeth could barely hear herself think.

"Didn't you hear a word Dad said this morning?" Elizabeth shouted over the blasting music. "This isn't just a vacation, you know. This week is supposed to help us get ready for college. It's about giving us motivation to get really serious about planning for our education and future."

"What?" Jessica shouted back.

"Jessica!" Elizabeth yelled. "Will you *please* turn that down?"

Jessica lowered the volume slightly.

"Thank you," Elizabeth said. "I was saying that this trip is not a vacation—it's really for planning our future."

"Right," Jessica agreed. "Like figuring out how to choose the perfect party to go to on Saturday night, how to secure fifty-yard-line seats at every home game, and how to find the best place to meet guys. Hey, maybe I'll even have a fling with some sexy professor. . . ." Jessica said, laughing. Elizabeth laughed along. She knew that Jessica was only joking—mostly. Unlike herself, Elizabeth knew, Jessica never really took anything academic too seriously.

"After all," Jessica continued, "if anyone deserves a great vacation, it's me—considering what a complete drain high school has been lately. I mean, to think that I was accused of cheating on the SATs when I couldn't care less about them in the first place." She wagged her finger at Elizabeth. "Like I'm not smart enough to do well on my own," she added indignantly. "You're not the only smart Wakefield twin, you know. We *do* share the same genes."

At the moment Elizabeth wasn't so sure about that last statement. While Elizabeth always considered the future, Jessica just lived for the present. And Elizabeth had absolutely no desire to prerush a sorority, or go to parties, in the coming week. She didn't have any desire to meet guys, either—not when she had a wonderful boyfriend back home.

"I just pray that I brought the right clothes," Jessica said. "I'd be so humiliated if my outfits reek of high school."

"What do high-school clothes smell like, anyway?" Elizabeth asked with a grin.

Jessica gave her sister an exasperated look. "I'm serious, Liz. How can I make a college guy fall in love with me if he thinks I'm a mere child?"

"Why are you so bent on making a college guy fall in love with you?" Elizabeth asked. "You have a wonderful boyfriend back home who's going to be pining away for you all week."

Jessica didn't respond. Instead she let out a whoop of delight. "Sweet Valley University—ten miles! Did you see that sign?"

"I guess I missed it," Elizabeth said.

"Good thing one of us is on the ball. We're almost there and you're falling asleep," she told her sister reproachfully, turning on her signal and switching lanes.

Elizabeth realized that Jessica was maneuvering the Jeep over to an exit ramp. "Where are we going?" she asked.

"I saw a sign for a minimart," Jessica explained. "We need to help Steven stock up on party provisions."

Elizabeth glanced at her sister, confused. "I don't remember Steven mentioning he was planning a party."

"He is now," Jessica shouted merrily over the blasting music.

"Jessica," Elizabeth told her sister patiently, "we can't just barge in on Steven and Billie and demand they throw a party in our honor."

"And why not?" Jessica asked with a smile. "It's not every day Steven gets to show off his two gorgeous sisters to all his college friends."

"Do you really think Steven would consider it an honor to introduce his kid sisters around?" Elizabeth asked. "And what about Billie?"

"Billie loves us!" Jessica argued.

"She's never had to live with us," Elizabeth reminded her sister. "Besides, knowing how thoughtful Billie is, she's probably already planned something for our first night."

"Well, then, they'll just have to change their plans." Jessica cranked up the stereo before Elizabeth could say anything in response.

Elizabeth sighed. There was no talking Jessica out of something once she'd made up her mind, and Elizabeth wasn't even going to try. It was clear that Jessica couldn't be dissuaded from viewing this trip as one big party. But Elizabeth also knew that Steven would sooner dye his hair blond than let his sisters use his apartment for a party. *And since I have no interest in throwing a party, I'm not going to help her convince him,* Elizabeth told herself firmly.

Jessica wandered the aisles of the store, piling her basket high with chips, dip, and soda. "I love nacho-cheese flavor!" she called, grabbing a bag of chips from a display. "Do you think we should get four bags?"

"Don't forget napkins and cups," Elizabeth added in a monotone, tossing the paper goods into the basket.

Jessica turned to look at her twin, surprised that she was helping. But the bored expression on Elizabeth's face told Jessica that her attitude had not improved. Jessica had been hoping that Elizabeth would feel the need to release some positive energy after the rigors of the last few weeks. But it seemed that Elizabeth was going to stick to being her normal stodgy self.

"Liz, we're not shopping for a wake," Jessica said. "You could at least *try* to get into the party spirit."

"I think you're providing all the party spirit this store needs," Elizabeth said glumly. "Any more would send the clerk running for safety."

Jessica scanned the store, noting the faraway glaze of the adolescent clerk chewing on a Slim Jim behind the counter. "Oh, right. This store is a regular party mobile," Jessica said with a laugh. She continued gathering supplies, grateful that at least Elizabeth wasn't stopping the shopping expedition outright.

They had just finished loading the bags into the back of the Jeep when Elizabeth decided she should use the rest room before they continued on to Steven and Billie's apartment.

"Can't it wait?" Jessica asked.

Elizabeth put her hands on her hips. "Jessica, I

helped you buy this stuff. The least you could do is give me a minute to use the bathroom."

"Fine," Jessica said, putting her hands in the pockets of her jeans and leaning back against the door of the Jeep. Elizabeth pivoted on her heel and marched back into the store to get the rest-room key.

Suddenly the roar of an engine invaded the calm of the parking lot. Jessica looked up to see an old Dodge Dart parking nearby. The car was overflowing with guys, and a couple of them were wearing SVU baseball caps. Jessica wasn't about to miss such a perfect opportunity.

Thinking fast, she rushed to the back of the Jeep and started fiddling with the trunk, pretending that she couldn't get the key out of the lock.

"This darn thing!" she swore as if to herself.

"Need some help with that?" a male voice called over to her.

"Um. I think I—" Jessica said, turning the key until she felt the lock catch. She didn't want any guy to think she was helpless, after all. "There, I got it!" she said, turning to face the owner of the voice. Jessica caught her breath as she saw the gorgeous young man in front of her. He was wearing a worn-out SVU sweatshirt that matched his bright-blue eyes, and he had a sexy display of stubble on his chin.

"Looks like you've got everything under control, then," the guy said with a laugh. "Too bad—I was hoping to be your hero."

"Who said you can't be my hero?" Jessica said,

smiling and tilting her head to one side so that he got a good look at the dimple in her left cheek. She knew that older men were suckers for dimples.

"Jake!" another male voice called out. "Are you bothering this fine specimen of womanhood?"

Jessica turned, thrilled to see a second gorgeous guy with mocha-brown skin and a flattop approaching the Jeep.

"Lay off, Phil. I spotted her first!" Jake said, putting an arm around Jessica's shoulders.

That move was a bit too forward, even for Jessica. "Guys! Guys! Easy now," Jessica said, pulling out from under Jake's arm. "No need to get all worked up here." She did love it when two guys competed for her attention, but they would have to play by her rules.

She looked into Jake's beautiful blue eyes. "Why don't we continue our conversation later? I'm planning a big party at my friend's apartment tonight."

"Cool!" said Jake.

Phil's eyes lit up. "All right!" he said enthusiastically.

"Be sure to tell all your friends," Jessica instructed, scribbling Steven's address on a gum wrapper she dug out of her purse.

"If you don't stop bothering that girl, you're going to be stranded out here!" the driver of the Dart yelled.

"We're coming, we're coming," Phil yelled back.

"You we'll see later," Jake told Jessica.

"I'm looking forward to it," she replied, and he returned to the other car.

The Dart was pulling out of the station by the time Elizabeth joined Jessica at the Jeep.

Phil stuck his head out of the back window. "Wow! Double the pleasure!" he yelled.

Jessica grinned wickedly. "Try double the trouble," she shouted back.

"Jess!" Elizabeth whispered. "Don't encourage them. You never know when you're flirting with the wrong guys," she said.

"Don't worry, Liz," Jessica said. "They were harmless." *I guess this isn't a good time to tell Liz they're coming to the party tonight*, Jessica thought wryly.

While waiting at a red light a few blocks away from Steven's apartment, Elizabeth noticed a parking lot full of plants and flowers. Wired to a chain-link fence was a crude sign: BUY A PLANT AND SEND A KID TO SUMMER CAMP—SPONSORED BY ZETA HOUSE.

"Look—some fraternity guys actually doing something useful with their Saturday afternoon," she observed.

"Frat guys? Where? Are they cute?" Jessica craned her neck around to get a good look.

"Over in that lot, selling plants to raise money for a worthy cause." Then a thought struck Elizabeth. "Oh, no! We completely forgot to get Steven and Billie a gift. Pull in."

"If you insist," Jessica said with a mischievous glint in her eyes. She steered the Jeep into an open parking place.

"This is silly," Jessica said as they were browsing through the rows of plants. "Who wants to worry about having to water something all the time?"

"Houseguests are always supposed to bring a gift," Elizabeth told her sister. "And considering this is our only option, a plant will have to do."

"We're not houseguests, Liz. We're Steven's *sisters,*" Jessica replied huffily.

"Sister and houseguest are not mutually exclusive, you know," Elizabeth said.

"Oh, right, I forgot I was dealing with Miss Manners's prize pupil," Jessica retorted.

Elizabeth laughed at Jessica's joke. "I just want us to get off on the right foot," she explained. "We're going to be disrupting their lives for a whole week."

"Spicing it up, is more like it," Jessica said.

Elizabeth decided to let that comment go. "Do you think they would like a fern?" she wondered aloud, spotting a lush green plant.

"Hey, check out what just rolled onto the lot," Jessica said. Elizabeth turned to look and saw a pickup truck pulling into the lot. The truck was loaded with plants, and two very good-looking guys sat in its cab.

"Maybe I'll go check out the new offerings," Jessica drawled, sauntering off toward the truck.

Elizabeth laughed and continued her search. Soon she had selected a healthy ficus tree and went looking for Jessica to help her carry it. Elizabeth wasn't surprised to find her sister right in her element: holding court in the middle of a group of guys.

"Jessica! Could you give me a hand over here?" Elizabeth yelled. Jessica looked up and waved dismissively, not moving from her spot. She seemed to be writing something on the back of one of the guys' hands.

Elizabeth shook her head and smiled. *For someone who has a boyfriend, Jessica sure is a flirt,* Elizabeth thought.

"Need some help?" a voice said suddenly from behind Elizabeth.

She turned to see an adorable guy with curly dark hair standing beside her. "Thanks," Elizabeth said, flashing him her sunniest smile. *If Jess can do it, so can I,* Elizabeth figured. *Besides, there's nothing wrong with a little innocent flirtation.*

"I don't know why we couldn't just have got a nice bouquet of flowers," Jessica grumbled when she noticed a smudge of brown soil marring her white jeans. The twins were finding that the ficus tree was a lot harder to get out of the backseat of the Jeep than it had been to get in. Especially since they no longer had the help of the frat guys.

"Plants last longer," Elizabeth responded reasonably.

"But why did you have to pick the biggest, bulkiest plant on the lot?" Jessica sighed.

"I remember Billie saying that she likes ficus trees," Elizabeth said. "Once we get it out of the backseat, we'll be fine."

"Yeah, we'll be just fine carrying it up three flights of stairs," Jessica said sarcastically. "I don't know why we don't just ring the bell and have Steven come help us."

"It's only two flights," Elizabeth corrected. "And it would be rude to make Steven deliver his own gift." She maneuvered her hands under the tree's big pot. "If we both lift at the same time, we can do it," she suggested. "Ready?"

"OK. One, two, three," Jessica prompted, and together they heaved. *It's no use,* Jessica realized as she lumbered toward the apartment building under the weight of the giant ficus. *Elizabeth won't listen to reason.*

Neither of them noticed that a man was walking out of the building until Jessica had already backed into him.

"Watch it!" he said brusquely.

"I'm sorry, sir," Elizabeth apologized. "My brother lives here, and we're just bringing him a plant."

"Lucky him," the man said sarcastically.

"Would you mind holding the door open?" Jessica asked.

The man let out a huge sigh. "Just don't make a mess on the stairs. One person slips, and I spend the rest of my life in court," he said, stalking off.

"I guess that's Steven's landlord," Elizabeth whispered.

"Oh, Steven's sure going to thank us for that one. What was that you said about being good houseguests?" Jessica asked.

"It's not our fault Steven's landlord is an old grouch," Elizabeth said, continuing toward the stairway. Then she gasped. "Watch out behind you!"

But the warning came too late. Jessica backed right into a recycling bin full of jars and cans. The crash of glass against metal made Jessica cringe. *Oops,* she thought sheepishly. In the hallway window next to her, a curtain jerked back and a sleepy face glared out to see what was causing the ruckus.

"And it's not our fault Steven's neighbors like to sleep in on the weekend," Jessica whispered out loud.

"Steven and Billie will love this, you'll see. C'mon, let's keep moving," Elizabeth ordered.

With half a flight to go, Jessica felt the pot slip out of her grasp. "Wait—it's slipping," she said. "I'm going to drop it if we don't put it down."

"Jess—"

"*Now!*" Jessica shouted, and they put the plant down. From above she heard someone call, "You think you could keep it quiet down there?"

"I'll tell you one thing," Jessica said with a laugh. "Steven better love this plant so much he's willing to carry it down two flights of stairs."

"What do you mean?" asked Elizabeth.

"Well, after he's been evicted—" Jessica began.

Elizabeth laughed, and Jessica smiled. *Looks like Liz might be lightening up a bit,* she thought. *Good. Maybe she actually won't get in the way of my good time.*

Chapter 3

Billie and Steven sat snuggled together on their lumpy brown velveteen sofa bed. Steven was lazily playing with Billie's silky chestnut hair as he concentrated on the history textbook on his lap. Billie was writing an outline for her philosophy paper in her notebook.

This was Steven's favorite way to study: alone with his girlfriend in their peaceful apartment. *I couldn't be more contented,* Steven thought, admiring Billie's delicate profile.

Suddenly a commotion out in the hallway interrupted the peace.

"Watch out for that railing!" Elizabeth's voice cried. Then there was a loud bang.

"Ouch!" Jessica yelped.

Both Steven and Billie broke into giggles. "The twins have definitely arrived," Steven said with a sigh.

He placed his pencil in his book to mark the page and got up off the couch.

Steven pulled open the door to reveal Elizabeth, standing with her fist raised, poised to knock. Jessica and a huge tree stood beside her.

"I guess you heard us coming," Jessica said, grinning.

"No, I have ESP," Steven said sarcastically.

"We brought you a plant," Elizabeth offered, smiling weakly.

"I noticed," Steven mumbled.

"Is that any way to welcome our guests?" Billie said. She pushed Steven out of the way and gave Elizabeth a warm hug. "It's gorgeous. And ficus trees are my favorite. Come on inside." She ushered the girls into the apartment, jabbing Steven lightly on his shoulder.

"Ow," Steven complained, rubbing his arm. "What was that for?"

"You were being rude to our guests," Billie said.

"Don't worry, Billie. We're used to it by now," Elizabeth said, smiling fondly at her brother. "After all, we've spent our whole lives dealing with Steven's rudeness."

"Oh, I get it," Steven said. "Now that I'm outnumbered, I'm the enemy."

"And you'd better not forget it!" Jessica teased, giving Steven a playful shove.

"Don't get me started, Jessica Wakefield." Steven shook his finger at her. She put up her hands in mock horror.

"OK, you two," Billie said. "Steven, bring that plant into the living room. I think it'll look great here between the couch and the bookcase."

"Yes, ma'am," Steven agreed.

Billie slapped her forehead. "I totally forgot to clear out some closet space for you in our bedroom," Billie told Jessica and Elizabeth. "Why don't you run downstairs and get your stuff. It won't take me long."

"Oh, you don't have to go through the trouble," Elizabeth said.

"Don't be silly," Billie said with a smile. "It's no big deal."

After the twins were settled in, Billie, Jessica, and Elizabeth rejoined Steven in the living room. Billie sat down next to Steven on the couch. "It was so thoughtful of you to bring a present," she said, admiring the plant in its new home. "I can tell right away that this will be different from our most recent experiences with houseguests."

"Why? What happened?" Elizabeth asked, balancing on one arm of the garish blue armchair.

Billie looked at Steven and they both groaned. "Let's see, where should I begin—?" Billie started.

"How about the long-distance calls your friend Suzanne racked up on our bill calling her boyfriend in Wisconsin?" Steven suggested with a frown.

"She promised she'd pay," Billie said, defending her friend.

"Have we seen a check?" Steven asked, crossing his arms over his chest and tapping one foot.

"OK, OK—wait," Billie said, erupting into giggles. "The crowning glory goes to our most recent guest: your buddy Oliver."

Steven groaned, putting a hand on his forehead. "You mean my *ex*-buddy Oliver. I was trying to forget about him."

"How can you? He just left last weekend," Billie said wearily.

"What did he do?" Elizabeth asked.

"What didn't he do?" Billie responded.

Steven elaborated. "First of all, he told me he just wanted to come for a weekend because he was considering transferring to SVU. Then it turned out that he had dropped out of school and had absolutely no plans. So he decided to make this a vacation—with free room and board courtesy of Steven and Billie. We finally kicked him out after three weeks."

Billie joined in. "He ate all our food, watched TV from dawn to dusk, smoked cigarettes like a chimney. I think it took a full five days for this place to stop smelling like an ashtray." She wrinkled her nose in disgust.

Steven shook his head. "He was using this place as party central, ruining our reputation with our neighbors. Our landlord even gave us a warning about the loud music." Steven took his girlfriend's hand in his own. "I don't think we had one moment of privacy the whole time he was here."

"Once I even caught him using my grandmother's vase as a beer mug!" Billie said, pointing to a beautiful antique vase on a shelf. "I've treasured that vase since I was twelve years old, when my family left Boston and she gave it to me as a keepsake." Billie turned to face the twins and smiled. "But I know you two would never act like that," she said.

Jessica, who was over at the bookshelf flipping through Steven and Billie's CD collection, didn't seem to be paying attention. All of a sudden a dozen CDs tumbled off the shelf. "Whoops!" Jessica cried, trying unsuccessfully to catch the falling CDs.

"At least Elizabeth wouldn't," Billie said, chuckling. "And she always keeps an eye on her sister." Elizabeth and Steven joined Billie's laughter.

"I'm a great guest," Jessica said defensively as she stacked the CDs in no particular order. She looked hurt when no one stopped laughing. "The tree was my idea," she ventured in her own defense.

Steven hooted. "Give me a break, Jess. You hate plants."

Jessica glared at him.

"When are you going to tell Steven and Billie about the idea that you *did* have?" Elizabeth prodded.

"Oh, right," said Jessica, turning to glare at her sister. She looked at Steven and opened her mouth. She paused and then jumped up. "Can we have lunch first? I'm starving!"

Steven watched Jessica disappear into the kitchen. *What is that sister of mine up to?* he thought worriedly.

* * *

"Do you have any more pickles?" Jessica asked as she examined the contents of the refrigerator.

"They should be right in the door," answered Billie. She was slicing tomatoes at the counter.

"This jar's empty," Jessica said, holding up a jar of pickle juice. Billie met Steven's eyes.

"Oliver!" they both cried.

"That's OK," Elizabeth said quickly. "We can do without."

"How about a cucumber?" Billie asked cheerily. "As my philosophy professor says, 'True satisfaction is attainable when one desires what is within reach.'"

Jessica felt like screaming. Philosophy, schmilosophy. *How can they actually be talking about classes on Saturday? It's the weekend, and weekends were invented to have fun and party with no distractions.*

"I hate cucumbers," grumbled Steven, taking another bite of his sandwich. The look on his face told Jessica that now would not be the best time to bring up her idea of having a party. Jessica looked at the kitchen clock. It was nearly one. If Steven and Billie didn't start calling all their friends to spread word about the party, the only people coming would be the guys Jessica had invited herself.

Although there was no one more adept at juggling multiple men than Jessica Wakefield, she had promised the guys that there would be a flock of girls at the party who were just as gorgeous as she was.

"Oh, I don't know how to tell you guys this. I

mean, I feel really awful, but . . ." Billie began.

"But what?" Elizabeth prompted her.

"Well, your genius brother didn't bother to tell me about your visit until late last night, and—"

"Wait a minute," Steven interjected. "I know I told you."

"Well, let's not get into that again," Billie said, patting Steven's arm. "Anyway, at the student union last week I saw a notice posted for a weekend special at a beachside bed-and-breakfast up the coast. And since we'd just suffered through three weeks of Oliver with barely a moment of privacy, I booked us a room to surprise Steven."

"When I, um, *reminded* Billie you two were coming, we tried to cancel, but we would have lost our deposit," Steven explained. "Do you mind fending for yourselves this weekend?" he asked.

Jessica raised an eyebrow. "Oh, I think we can manage," she said, trying not to smile too broadly.

"Don't worry about us," Elizabeth said. "We'll find something to do to entertain ourselves, right, Jess?"

Jessica nodded, almost unable to believe her good luck.

"I would hate to be the ones who made you sacrifice a much-deserved getaway weekend," Elizabeth continued, "especially after all the houseguest nightmares you've just been through."

"Thanks for understanding," Billie said. "We could really use a break."

"Would you mind not telling Mom and Dad?" Steven asked. "Dad just gave me a long lecture about being your responsible older brother, and I don't know how understanding he would be if he found out I was leaving you alone on your first weekend here."

"Oh, no, not Ned Wakefield's dreaded responsibility lecture," Jessica said. She had got the same lecture so many times herself, she could practically recite it word for word.

Elizabeth smiled at Steven. "You're right—it's probably best not to tell Mom and Dad. They're likely to get all worried over nothing," Elizabeth said.

"We wouldn't dream of getting you in trouble," Jessica agreed. *I couldn't have planned it better myself,* she thought with glee. *With Steven and Billie gone, my path is completely clear to throw a raging college party!*

"And you can count on us to take good care of the apartment," Elizabeth said. "You won't even know we were here." Elizabeth looked her sister straight in the eye.

Jessica returned her stare and smiled. *Well, there's still one obstacle in my path,* she reminded herself.

"Looks like your party idea is out. Oh, well," Elizabeth said after Billie and Steven had left. She was relieved that Jessica hadn't even had the chance to broach the subject with Steven. Steven probably would have been so annoyed with Jessica's crazy idea that he might have blamed Elizabeth for it, too. She didn't want to risk getting thrown out of his apartment before the week had even started.

Elizabeth picked up the current issue of the campus newspaper lying on the kitchen table. "I bet we can find something interesting happening on campus tonight," she said, flipping to the back to look at the events listings. "Let's see. . . . There's a poetry reading at the student union," she suggested.

"I think not," Jessica replied coldly.

"Right, I guess that's more my type of activity than yours." Elizabeth scanned the pages for more options. "How about a silent-film festival? Those can be fun in a silly sort of way."

"Sounds like a blast," Jessica said in a tone of absolute boredom.

Elizabeth flipped to the next page. "OK, I was trying to broaden your horizons a bit, but I think I found something more up your alley: a jazz trio at the local coffee bar."

"Dullsville," Jessica sighed.

Elizabeth tossed the paper aside in frustration. "OK, Miss Veto Queen. Let's hear you come up with some suggestions."

"Well, since you ask . . ." Jessica started hesitantly. "I don't know why we have to rule out the party idea."

"Are you out of your mind?" Elizabeth asked sharply. "Throw a party in Steven and Billie's apartment while they're out of town? Steven would *kill* us."

"Not if he doesn't know," Jessica said. She arched her eyebrows questioningly at her twin.

"No! No way, Jess." Elizabeth stood up and turned to face her sister. "I'm surprised that even you would consider doing something like that behind Steven's back. We're not having a party, and you're just going to have to deal with it." Elizabeth watched as Jessica's pout became more pronounced. "It's not the end of the world, Jess," Elizabeth continued. "You go to parties all the time."

"But they're not *college* parties," Jessica whined.

"I don't care," Elizabeth replied. "There's no way we're throwing a party tonight."

Jessica bit her lip and opened her mouth as if to say something. She looked furtively around the room.

Elizabeth eyed her sister with dread. She knew her twin's look—it was the Jessica-is-up-to-something look. "What?" she demanded, thrusting her hands on her hips.

"Well," Jessica said tentatively, "I kind of already told some people that we were having a party here tonight."

Elizabeth gasped. "You did what? Who did you tell? Who could you have possibly invited already?"

"Remember those nice guys at that place we bought the plant?" Jessica asked. "Them."

"Oh, that's what you were doing," Elizabeth said, slapping a hand to her forehead. "And I thought you were just flirting. Well, that's not the end of the world. They were all from Zeta House, so you can just call over there and tell them the party's been canceled," Elizabeth concluded reasonably.

"I can't do that," Jessica cried. "I'd be humiliated!"

"You'll get over it," Elizabeth said, tapping one foot.

"But they're planning their Saturday night around this party," Jessica argued.

Elizabeth sat on the sofa and crossed her arms over her chest. "They'll just have to figure out something else to do," she said darkly. "Besides, there are probably about a million other parties going on tonight."

"Well . . ." Jessica said. "I also told some other people."

"Who?"

"There were those gorgeous guys I met at the minimart while you were in the rest room," Jessica explained. "And I have no idea how to get in touch with them."

"I can't believe you invited those guys!" Elizabeth exclaimed. "You don't know anything about them."

"I know they go to SVU and that they're totally cute," Jessica said.

"And when they show up," Elizabeth responded flatly, "you'll just have to tell them there's no party."

"What was I thinking?" Jessica said in a huff. "I thought maybe since we were at college, you wouldn't be the worrywart stick-in-the-mud you always are. Clearly, I was wrong."

"We're not in college, Jess," Elizabeth said patiently. "We're just visiting."

"C'mon, Liz," Jessica pleaded. "I promise I'll keep it small. Just us, those guys, and a couple of their friends. It'll be fun."

Elizabeth looked at her sister's plaintive pout and puppy-dog eyes and groaned. The thought of sitting in Steven's apartment all night, turning away people who showed up for the party, sounded like about as much fun as watching the ficus tree take root in its new home.

She *could* just go to campus by herself, do something she really wanted to do, and let Jessica deal with turning people away. *But knowing Jessica, with me out of the house, she'd just go ahead with the party,* Elizabeth realized. *And that could be a complete disaster.* She hated it when Jessica backed her into a corner like this. But what choice did she have?

"OK, you can have the party if you keep it small," Elizabeth said finally. "But I mean small!"

Jessica's face lit up. "You're the best, Liz," she squealed, running over to give Elizabeth a hug.

"And since I don't want to be on Steven and Billie's list of houseguest nightmares," Elizabeth began, "I won't tell them—"

"Thank you, thank you, thank you!" Jessica gushed.

"—*if* you promise to clean up. And I mean sparkling clean," Elizabeth concluded firmly.

"I promise," Jessica said.

"I mean it, Jess—I'm not lifting a finger," Elizabeth warned her twin.

"OK, OK, I got the message," Jessica said. "In fact, why don't I start by putting away some of this clutter so it doesn't get in the way?" She jumped up and started throwing candlesticks, magazines, and knickknacks into a hall cupboard.

Elizabeth rolled her eyes and looked up toward the ceiling. *Please tell me this isn't going to be another one of Jessica's huge mistakes.*

Chapter 4

"I can't see any address, but the last house we passed was two forty-two, so this has got to be two forty-four," Billie said, craning her neck to look out the car window. They had pulled up in front of an ancient Victorian house with peeling white paint and faded green shutters. "Do you see a sign anywhere?"

"I think I see something hanging on that post." Steven inched the car a few feet forward. "Hilda's Tavern," he read out loud.

"That's weird," Billie said. "Right address, wrong place." Just then a woman dressed in an apron appeared from the side of the house. She walked onto the porch and started watering one of the many hanging vines with an old-fashioned watering can.

"Excuse me, miss!" Billie called out to the woman.

The woman looked up. "Can I help you, dearie?"

"We're looking for Carla's Cottage on the Coast," Billie replied. "Do you know where it is?"

"You've found it," the woman said with a jolly cackle. "You must be Billie Winkler."

"Yes, I am," Billie called back.

"Well, don't just sit there in your car all day. Come on in and get yourselves settled! We've been expecting you." The woman disappeared into the house, letting the screen door slam shut behind her.

Steven and Billie looked at each other and shrugged. "I guess this is it," Steven said. He drove into the dirt parking lot on the side of the house. There was one other car in the lot.

Billie peered at the house. "Oh, Steven, this looks awful," she said. "It looked so cute in the brochure."

Steven glanced at the drawing on the cover of the brochure in Billie's hand. "I think the illustrator took some artistic liberties," he said, laughing softly. "But it's really not that bad. With a good paint job it would look as pretty as its picture."

Billie chuckled. "I'm not so sure about that," she said. She looked at Steven with sad eyes. "I'm sorry, sweetie. I really wanted this weekend to be perfect."

"I know," Steven said consolingly. During the ride up, Billie had been second-guessing herself about the weekend, wondering whether they should have canceled so they could stay home with the twins. Steven had to keep on reassuring his girlfriend that a weekend at a charming bed-and-breakfast was a great idea, and besides, it would have been silly to waste the deposit money.

"It can still be perfect," Steven said now. "So what if the place isn't the most beautiful bed and breakfast in the world? I'll bet our room is really cute and charming."

Billie laughed and gave him a playful shove. "You're right. C'mon, let's bring in our stuff."

The woman was waiting for them behind a large oak desk in the entranceway. "So you must be Carla," Steven said as the woman began checking them in.

"No, Carla's my daughter," the woman responded.

"Then who's Hilda?" he asked.

"You're looking at her." Hilda looked up at their confused faces. "Oh, you're probably wondering about that sign out front." She put her hand on her chin. "I've got to remember to take that down. But it's nailed on so gosh-darn tight, I almost gave myself a hernia trying to pull it off," she said with a snort. She looked Steven up and down. "You look like a strong young fellow. Could you do old Hilda a huge favor and take down that sign?"

Steven glanced at Billie, who raised her eyebrows and gave him an amused smile. "Um, sure," he said.

"Oh, lovely," Hilda gushed, clapping her hands together. "And while you're at it, would you mind sticking up this one?" From behind the desk she pulled out a sign that had the words CARLA'S COTTAGE ON THE COAST hand-painted on it. "That sounds much more romantic than 'Hilda's Tavern,' doesn't it?" Hilda asked. "My Carla, she's a bright girl."

"No problem," Steven replied weakly.

After they had finished checking in, Steven and Billie brought their luggage upstairs. They stopped in front of a door with the number 4 messily stenciled on it. "Here's ours," Steven said. "You watch—I bet it's adorable." He pushed the door open to reveal a tiny attic room with a single twin bed, a lumpy couch, and a plywood dresser that was missing its top drawer. The ceiling had a gigantic water stain spread across its length, and the wallpaper was a dingy avocado color with a pattern of purple roses.

"Oh, no! This room is about as romantic as a phone booth!" Billie exclaimed. She went to the bed and flopped down with a bang. "Ow!" She stood up, massaging her rear. She lifted the bedspread to find that the bed was no more than a four-inch-thick foam mattress lying on top of a wooden platform.

"This is just awful, Steven," Billie said sadly. "I can't believe I was taken in by that stupid offer."

"Stop beating yourself up, Billie," Steven said, gently putting his arm around his girlfriend. "It was a wonderful idea and an honest mistake."

"But I dragged you all the way here, leaving poor Jessica and Elizabeth all on their own."

"Oh, I think my sisters are quite capable of taking care of themselves for a couple of days," Steven said. "Let's just unpack and explore the town."

Billie looked around the room. "Where's the bathroom?"

"I guess we have to use the one on the floor downstairs," Steven figured.

"This just keeps getting worse and worse!" Billie lamented.

"We're going to have a wonderful weekend," Steven said gently, stroking a strand of hair from Billie's face. He pulled her close, wrapping her tightly in his arms. Over Billie's head, Steven stared at the garish water stain on the ceiling. It looked fresh. That wasn't a reassuring sight, but if he didn't keep a positive attitude, Billie would feel even worse.

"I love this place," he said out loud, looking straight into her eyes. "I love you." He cupped Billie's face in his hands and kissed her tenderly. *This isn't quite the weekend we imagined, but I'm determined to enjoy myself,* Steven decided. *For Billie's sake.*

Elizabeth had decided to wander around campus and enjoy the warm, sunny afternoon. Jessica had insisted on heading straight for the student dormitories, so they decided to start at Dickenson Hall, which was one of the largest.

But now they were lost in the middle of campus. Throngs of students rushed past, but everyone was walking so quickly, and with such purpose, Elizabeth didn't want to bother them to ask for directions. Then she spotted a girl standing to the side, shuffling through her book bag. Elizabeth jogged over to her and asked, "Do you know the way to Dickenson Hall?"

The girl looked up and did a double take when she saw the identical blondes standing in front of her. "Sorry, you startled me," the girl said, blushing.

"It's OK, we're used to it," Jessica said, laughing.

"You're almost at Dickenson," the girl said, pointing her arm out in the direction they were heading. "It's just around to the back of the life-sciences building."

"Thanks," Elizabeth said, and she and Jessica continued walking.

Just as the girl had said, they found Dickenson Hall the moment they rounded the corner of the life-sciences building. The dormitory was modern and multistoried, with a lush green expanse of grass in front. Throngs of students bustled in and out of the front entrance, waving hellos, calling up to their friends who leaned out of open windows. Dueling stereos blasted music out over the lawn. On one side of the building, Beethoven's Fifth Symphony drowned out all other music. On the other side, a popular dance beat prevailed.

Flags and banners hung from several windows, some of them simply advertising their owners' allegiance to their fraternity or sorority, others making political statements. One simply read, "You gotta fight for the right to party!"

Elizabeth glanced at her sister to see how the scene was affecting her. Jessica looked as awestruck as Elizabeth felt. "Can you imagine living in this place?" Elizabeth gushed.

"I was just thinking the same thing. It's like one big party," Jessica said excitedly. "Let's take a walk through the halls."

"Jess, this is their home," Elizabeth protested. "We can't just barge in uninvited."

"Don't be ridiculous," Jessica said dismissively. "No one's going to mind." She charged for the front entrance, not even waiting for Elizabeth to try to stop her. Elizabeth sighed and trotted after her sister.

Wandering through the halls, Jessica peeked into the many open doors. Everyone seemed to be having a party in his or her room. There were young people just hanging out and talking; some were putting up posters or checking out each other's CD collections; others looked as if they were involved in some pretty lively group-study sessions. *I guess not everyone knows what college is really about,* Jessica thought.

Suddenly Jessica almost barreled into a guy wearing nothing but boxer shorts. "Oh, excuse me," he said, giving her an appreciative look up and down.

Jessica flashed her brightest smile. "No, it's my fault, really. I wasn't looking where I was going," she said, trying not to drool over his washboard stomach.

"You shouldn't have to, gorgeous. We should all stop and stare when you walk down the hall," he said smoothly. Then he noticed Elizabeth standing two steps behind Jessica. "What's this?" he asked. "There are two of you?"

"We were just visiting," Elizabeth explained. "I

hope you don't mind us wandering around your dorm."

"Mind?" he asked. "Why would I mind? Girls as gorgeous as you two are welcome here anytime. I'm sorry I'm not more presentable, but I was on my way to the bathroom." He turned and continued walking down the hall.

Jessica watched him disappear into an open doorway. *Wait!* she wanted to call after him. *Who are you? I want to invite you to my party!* She grabbed Elizabeth's arm. "Aren't coed dorms the coolest?" she asked her twin. "Imagine having boys around every minute of the day."

"I don't know," Elizabeth said. "I think I'd be kind of self-conscious."

"Give me a break! What's there to be self-conscious about?" Jessica asked, thinking about how much fun it would be to parade around in her sexiest nightgowns, making all the guys drool.

The twins made their way down the hall, past the wide-open door the guy had just entered. The scene inside stopped Jessica and Elizabeth in their tracks. The guy in the boxer shorts stood in front of a long line of sinks. He was drooling, all right—white toothpaste foam dribbled down his chin as he vigorously brushed his teeth. A girl in a sweatsuit stood at the next sink over, peering and poking at a zit on her nose.

Jessica caught her breath. "I didn't know they had to share bathrooms," she whispered.

"Coed dorms aren't so glamorous, after all," Elizabeth said, laughing.

"Let's give them some privacy," Jessica decided. She turned to continue down the hallway.

Now that she was inside the dormitory, Elizabeth didn't feel like an intruder. The students seemed to be casual about their personal space—most of the doors were wide-open. She didn't want to snoop, but she was so curious about dormitory life that she couldn't stop herself from peeking into the rooms. Most of the students seemed to be just hanging out and talking, but in a lot of rooms, Elizabeth was happy to see students engaged in serious study sessions.

Letting her twin walk on ahead, Elizabeth paused in front of a room where four students were sitting on the floor, surrounded by books and papers. "Well, then, Mr. History Expert," one of the girls in the room asked, "what would *you* consider to be the most important outcome of the Treaty of Versailles?" Elizabeth moved on. Although she enjoyed studying history, it wasn't really her favorite subject.

In the next room she heard two students engaged in a heated discussion of literature, which was right up Elizabeth's alley. "I don't agree with you," a pretty African-American girl said. "I think that Zora Neale Hurston has had a more profound influence on modern black literature than Ralph Ellison."

Her companion gasped. "Are you out of your

mind?" he exclaimed. "Ellison's *Invisible Man* revolutionized the way blacks view their own identity!"

"Maybe that's true for black men, but I think a lot of black women would say the same thing about *Their Eyes Were Watching God,*" the girl argued.

"Oh, now you're going to turn this into a sexist thing? Forget it!" The boy threw his pen down onto the floor. Elizabeth smiled as she watched their argument continue to gain momentum. *I can't wait for the opportunity to live with other students who actually enjoy sitting around and talking about literature, history, and social issues*, she thought.

Suddenly the girl looked up and noticed Elizabeth standing in the doorway. "What do you think?" she asked Elizabeth.

"I haven't read either book," Elizabeth admitted. "So I really don't think I should offer my opinion on—"

"That doesn't matter," the girl interrupted. "I'd like to know how you feel. Do you think black men can speak for black women?"

Before Elizabeth could answer the question, Jessica shouted to her from down the hall. "Liz! Are you coming?"

"Um," Elizabeth stammered, looking from the expectant faces of the students in the room to her sister's impatient face down the hall. "Did you want to move on?" Elizabeth called out to Jessica.

"It's OK," Jessica said, waving her hand at her twin. "I'll just go on by myself. What do you say we meet back here in about half an hour?"

"Oh. Sure, Jess," Elizabeth said. She turned back to the girl in the room. "Are you sure it's OK if I come in and join your conversation?" she asked.

"Of course," the girl said. As Elizabeth stepped into the room and took a seat on the bed, the girl asked her, "Have you read Alice Walker's *The Color Purple*? Now, that book completely proves my point. . . ."

Jessica watched her sister disappear into the open doorway. *Perfect,* she said to herself. *With Elizabeth all caught up in a discussion, I'm free to spread the word about the party.* Finding students to come to her party was the reason Jessica had wanted to come to the dormitories in the first place. Billie had mentioned that news travels faster in college dormitories than over the Internet, and Jessica wanted to put that idea to the test. She just had to make sure that Elizabeth didn't see her inviting more people.

Suddenly Jessica was enveloped by the unmistakable aromas of popcorn and nail polish. The smell seemed to be coming from a room that was also blasting Jamie Peters—Jessica's favorite singer. She approached the doorway and saw three girls doing their nails. "Now, this is a gorgeous room," Jessica said, staring at the Jamie Peters posters that were plastered all over the walls.

A pretty girl with bright-red hair glanced up at

Jessica. "Thank you," she said pleasantly. "Are you looking for someone?"

"No," Jessica replied. "I was just admiring your taste in artwork." She grinned and took a step into the room.

The girls laughed. "Jamie Peters was born a work of art," the blond girl said, a dreamy look in her eyes.

"Well, come on in," the redheaded girl said to Jessica. "Do you want to try out my new nail polish? It's called Tangerine Dream."

"Sure!" Jessica responded enthusiastically. She entered the room and sat down next to a girl with long chestnut-brown hair. "Pass the buffer, please."

By the time ten minutes had passed, Jessica knew that this group of girls was exactly her type. And for the icing on the cake, Darcy, the redhead, had just pledged to Theta Alpha Theta. *Bumping into Darcy today must be an omen,* Jessica thought happily. *I just know I'm destined to be a Theta.*

Before Jessica moved on, she told the three girls, "I'm throwing a party at my brother Steven's place tonight and I'd love it if you came. And don't be shy about telling your friends—so far the only people I've got coming are guys!"

"My kind of party!" the blond girl cheered. Then Darcy suggested that Jessica post a notice about the party on the bulletin board in the dorm's entranceway.

"What a great idea," Jessica told Darcy with a smile. "I'll go do that right now." She said her good-byes to the girls and set off to put up the notice.

Jessica had just tacked up a small sign when she heard Elizabeth's voice a few feet away. *I can't let Liz see this notice,* Jessica thought with a flicker of panic. *She'd rip it down so fast, the bulletin board would get whiplash.* She managed to block the party notice with her body just as her sister came around the corner.

Elizabeth and an attractive African-American girl stopped a few feet away from Jessica. "Well, it was great meeting you," Elizabeth said, shaking the girl's hand. "Maybe I'll bump into you later on this week."

The girl waved and headed out the door, a huge backpack strapped over her shoulder.

"Didn't you invite her to our party?" Jessica asked, keeping herself strategically between Elizabeth and the bulletin board.

"Oh, Jess!" Elizabeth said, turning to face her twin. "I was so involved in conversation, I didn't even see you there." She frowned. "And *no,* I did not invite her to the party," she said in an exasperated tone. "We agreed to keep it small, remember?" Then she narrowed her eyes. "Jessica Wakefield, please don't tell me you went around inviting everyone in the dorm to Steven's apartment tonight!"

"Of course not," Jessica replied innocently.

"I sure hope not," Elizabeth said, still staring at her sister suspiciously.

"Are you ready to go?" Jessica asked. She felt proud of the nonchalant tone of her question. *Sometimes I'm such a good actress, I scare myself,* she thought, waiting for Elizabeth to turn away before she moved from her place in front of the bulletin board. Luckily, Elizabeth swiveled and headed straight for the door.

As they walked down the path leading out of the dorm, the blond girl from the room with all the Jamie Peters posters scooted past them on in-line skates.

"Hey, Jessica! See you tonight!" the blond girl called back over her shoulder. Jessica felt the angry glare of her sister, but she ignored it. *There isn't anything my bossy sister can do now,* she thought happily. *Tonight Steven's apartment will be home to the most rocking party Sweet Valley U has ever seen.*

"So," Steven asked Billie, "what should we do on our first day of vacation?"

Billie smiled and hooked her arm through his. "Let's walk around town for a while," she suggested. "Maybe we'll find a nice romantic restaurant to come back to for dinner."

But they soon found out that the number of romantic spots in town was extremely limited. The tiny main street boasted a hardware store, a post office, a greasy diner, and a deli. There was a cute-looking Italian restaurant, but it had a big sign in its window that read CLOSED FOR VACATION. The restaurant looked as if it hadn't been opened in years.

"No wonder Hilda's is the only inn in town," Billie

said. "The place has about as much tourist appeal as Antarctica."

Steven laughed. "Well, it does have the beach."

Billie squeezed his arm. "Oh, right. So, Steven, how about a big bowl of seaweed for dinner?"

Chapter 5

"Great party!" Jeff shouted to Jessica over the blasting music. He was bobbing and bouncing to a rhythm all his own, and every time he shouted, he leaned right into Jessica's face, his breath reeking of sour-cream-and-onion potato chips.

"Thanks," Jessica said, trying not to gag. She had almost melted with delight when the gorgeous fraternity jock had asked her to dance. Too bad Jeff was turning out to have about as much personality as his wrinkled button-down shirt, and as much rhythm as an ironing board. Luckily, the song ended, so Jessica could excuse herself to change the CD.

Aside from the lameness of her last dance partner, Jessica couldn't help but give herself an enthusiastic pat on the back for how well the party was going. As she surveyed the room, she was pleased to see that everyone was having a great time. Even Elizabeth was talking and laughing.

A big group of guys from Zeta House had shown up at exactly the same time Jessica's new friend Darcy from Dickenson Hall had arrived with a bunch of girls from Theta House. The two large groups had sent the atmosphere immediately into a festive party mode.

Now Jessica looked over at Darcy and her friends. She hadn't figured Darcy to be such a flashy dresser from the sweats she had been wearing in her room, but Jessica was pleased that Darcy had shown up looking terrific in a flouncy miniskirt and thigh-highs. Each one of the Thetas had at least two guys hanging on to her every word. The Thetas were the best-dressed, the prettiest, the most charming, and the most popular girls at the party. Jessica walked over to their group. "Are you guys having fun?" she asked.

"Great party!" Darcy replied enthusiastically. "Jess, I'd like you to meet a couple of our sisters from Theta House: Amanda Gregory and Magda Helperin."

"I'm so glad you could come," Jessica said graciously.

"Thanks for inviting us," Amanda said. Amanda was a slender, energetic girl with bleached-blond hair cut in a short bob.

Magda held out a hand for Jessica to shake. "I understand you're Alice Wakefield's daughter," she drawled.

"Yes, I am," Jessica answered, thinking that Magda's velvety voice perfectly matched her appearance. With her crystal-blue eyes, fair skin, and glossy black hair, she reminded Jessica of a fairy-tale princess. Her gold silk blouse made her look even more like royalty. Jessica liked her immediately.

"Jessica, you should come to the house sometime to get better acquainted with Theta Alpha Theta," Magda said.

"I'd love to!" Jessica gushed.

"Why don't you come for afternoon tea?" Darcy suggested. "Are you free on Monday?"

Jessica beamed. "I'll make myself free."

"Well then, how about two thirty?" Darcy asked.

Jessica was elated. She knew that these very girls would be juniors and seniors by the time she was a freshman. When it came time for her to rush, they would be the ones to decide whether or not she was Theta material.

If Jessica was going to have any future in college at all, she had to belong to the best sorority on campus. And that was Theta, obviously. *This next week could make my future . . . or break it,* Jessica thought. *I can't do anything wrong, and I have to do absolutely everything right.*

Elizabeth's heart sank as the doorbell rang again. And again. Each time it rang, Jessica herded more people into Steven's apartment, which was now bursting to overflowing. *This is getting completely out of hand,* Elizabeth realized.

She walked over to Jessica, who was at the stereo fiddling with the equalizer. "Do you think many more people will be showing up?" Elizabeth asked.

"Do I look like a psychic?" Jessica replied, plopping five new CDs onto the carousel. "Parties have a life of their own, Liz. You just have to sit back, relax, and see where this one goes."

"You don't have to be so snippy," Elizabeth replied. "It's just that the apartment seems to be filling up, and I don't want things to get too crowded." Then she added, "And we're running out of toilet paper."

Jessica laughed so hard, she let out an involuntary snort. "Stop worrying and enjoy yourself for once in your life," Jessica told her sister. "Next thing I know, you'll be running out to get more dental floss."

Elizabeth sighed as Jessica turned her attention back to the stereo. *It looks like I'm the only one worried about keeping this party under control,* Elizabeth thought. *It just better not get too crazy—there's only so much I can do alone.*

While pouring more punch into the bowl, Jessica mentally ran through the different outfits she'd packed. She was trying to figure out what to wear for her tea date at Theta House. Her black palazzo pants paired with a flowing cream silk top? Or maybe a more fun look: her tight red T-shirt dress. *No, too racy,* Jessica decided. Then she thought of the perfect outfit: her teal two-piece linen suit. *Good thing I packed it,* she thought happily.

A popular dance beat started its hypnotic bass line, and everyone jumped up to dance. Jessica was just breaking open a new bag of chips when out of the corner of her eye she noticed someone knock into the vase Billie's grandmother had given her. Jessica ran to catch it, but before she arrived, a pair of big, strong hands rescued the delicate vase.

Breathing a deep sigh of relief, she looked up at a guy who had the greenest eyes she'd ever seen. "How can I ever thank you?" she gushed, taking the vase from his hands.

"You might want to put this somewhere where it'll be safe," he suggested. His voice was smooth and sexy, perfectly suited to his clean-cut, boyish good looks.

"Good idea," Jessica said brightly. "And your name is—?"

"Zach. Zach Marsden," he said, holding out his hand.

"Jessica Wakefield," she said, switching the vase to her left arm so she could shake hands. He held her grip a few seconds longer than necessary, staring intently into her face with his breathtakingly beautiful eyes. *I could live, breathe, and eat in these eyes forever,* Jessica thought rapturously.

"That's a gorgeous vase," Zach said finally, breaking the spell. "Is it an heirloom?"

"My grandmother gave it to me when my parents

moved my family here from Boston," Jessica answered without stopping to think.

"You grew up in Boston?" Zach asked. "How old were you when you moved here?"

"Um . . . twelve," Jessica replied haltingly. *Now why in the world did I start this story?* she wondered.

"I'm from the East Coast myself," Zach said.

Jessica smiled. *So that's why I said I'm from the East Coast,* she realized. *It's my intuitive mind at work again. Now we have something in common.*

"I'm a junior in college back there," Zach continued. "But I wanted a taste of California life. So I transferred here for a semester."

"And what do you think of California so far?" Jessica asked, gazing at Zach through her long lashes.

"I love it!" he replied enthusiastically. "And it's looking even better now that I've met Jessica Wakefield."

Jessica beamed. *With a smile like that,* she thought, *I'll pretend I'm from Bora Bora if it means I have something in common with Zach Marsden!*

"You want to put that vase away somewhere?" he asked. Jessica looked down to see that she was still cradling the vase in her arm. *Who knew this stupid vase would turn out to be a love totem?* she thought happily.

Elizabeth was washing her hands in the bathroom sink when the banging started. "Just a minute," Elizabeth called through the bathroom door.

The banging got louder. "Hurry up in there!" said a gruff voice. "We've got precious cargo out here." Someone kicked the bottom of the door.

"OK, OK, I'm coming," Elizabeth said, annoyed. She yanked the door open and gasped. Three burly guys stood in front of her, and they were holding a frosty keg of beer.

"What are you doing?" Elizabeth cried.

"What do you think, honey? Move over so we can put this down." One of the guys shoved past her, dropping the keg into the shower.

"You can't put that in here!" Elizabeth blurted, not knowing what else to say.

"We just did," one of the guys replied, grinning to reveal a chipped front tooth. "Hey, Skip! Hand over the tap."

Infuriated, Elizabeth set off to hunt for Jessica and found her talking to a preppy-looking guy by the food table. "Did you let those guys with the keg into the apartment?" she asked her sister angrily.

"I don't know," Jessica said breezily, turning her back on Elizabeth. "I guess *someone* let them in."

Elizabeth grabbed her twin by one shoulder and swung her around so that they were face-to-face. "We can't have a keg in here, Jessica," Elizabeth said through clenched teeth. "I bet there isn't a single person here who's over twenty-one!"

"Lighten up, Liz," Jessica said with a laugh. "This is a *college* party. Everyone drinks at college parties—it's totally normal."

"There's nothing normal about underage drinking," Elizabeth argued. "A lot of people drove here!"

"Fine, you want to get rid of the keg?" Jessica snorted. Elizabeth nodded forcefully. "Be my guest," Jessica continued. "All you have to do is carry it out."

"That's just what I'll do," Elizabeth replied. But when she walked back to the bathroom, she was dismayed to see that a crowd of people had already discovered the arrival of the keg. *Like bees to honey,* Elizabeth observed. The crowd outside the bathroom was so thick, she couldn't even walk through the hall. She watched with horror as they fought and pushed to get to the beer.

"My turn!" one guy called. "I'm next."

"No, me," the girl next to him replied.

Another girl edged her way closer to the keg. "You just filled your cup!" she complained.

"All I got was foam!" the first girl answered.

They would riot if I tried to drag it out, Elizabeth realized. She was too late.

Jessica couldn't worry about the keg—she was too engrossed in her conversation with Zachary Marsden. She couldn't stop talking and flirting with him.

"I'm surprised—and disappointed—that I haven't met you sooner," Zach said. "It's a pretty small campus, and with that beautiful blond hair, you're definitely someone I would have noticed. The fact that I've been living on the same campus as Jessica Wakefield for months drives me crazy," he said.

"I know it must've been hard, but it looks like you've survived with flying colors," Jessica said with a playful grin on her face. Zach was clearly under the impression that she was a student at SVU. And why shouldn't he have that impression? She was just as sophisticated as any college girl—probably even more sophisticated. *What's the harm in letting him believe I'm in college?* she decided. *I'm only going to be here for a week, anyway.*

But she had to come up with a reasonable explanation for why he had never seen her around campus. After all, he was right: If Jessica Wakefield had been on the campus of Sweet Valley University for more than a day, every male student would have known about it.

I know, Jessica thought, pleased with her ingenuity. *I'll say I'm a transfer student, too!* "Actually, there's a reason you haven't seen me on campus before," she said out loud.

"What's that?"

"I just transferred here myself from back east," she said. "Isn't that a total coincidence?"

"Get out!" Zach exclaimed. "Where'd you transfer from?"

Whoops! Jessica thought. *I forgot to think of a school.* "Princeton," she blurted, the name popping out of her mouth almost involuntarily. Jessica knew instantly why that name had come to her. Princeton was not only the name of an eastern university, it was also where the company that put out the SATs was located. In the past few weeks Jessica had seen the return address on more envelopes than she cared to remember. *I never wanted to think about that miserable place again,* she thought with a silent groan.

"No way! Beautiful and smart, too," Zach said appreciatively. "Princeton's a top-notch school. I didn't even apply because I knew I wouldn't get in."

She smiled at Zach. "Yes, well, when you've got it, you've got it," she said, now glad that she had said Princeton. She wanted Zach to know right away that her looks were not the only thing she had going for her. College guys liked girls who could hold deep and meaningful conversations.

"I have some friends who are freshmen at Princeton," Zach said. "Let's see . . . do you know Steve Markman?" Jessica shook her head. "Jerome Silver? Noelle Lam?"

Jessica shook her head. "It's a big school," she offered.

"Not really," Zach said, looking puzzled.

"I mean, I wasn't there that long, so I didn't get much of a chance to get to know a lot of people," she explained.

"That makes sense," Zach said, reaching for a can of soda. "So why did you leave? Princeton's a great school, and a beautiful town." He pulled the tab and took a swig, giving Jessica ample opportunity to admire the arc of his smooth neck as he leaned his head back. She imagined kissing that neck, rubbing her fingers over his broad shoulders, seeking his lips with her own. Then she noticed he was looking at her expectantly. *Oh, right, he's waiting for me to answer his question,* she thought distractedly.

"I thought I missed life on the East Coast," she said out loud. "But I found out right away that I'm a true California transplant. I missed it here too much."

"But in the middle of the semester? Wasn't it hard to get your credits transferred?" Zach asked.

"Oh, they gave me a little trouble at first," Jessica said, twirling a lock of blond hair around her finger. "But then I convinced them that they needed me as a student more than I needed their stupid credits."

"I'm sure that convinced them," Zach said with a laugh.

This story is going over quite easily, Jessica thought with a self-satisfied grin. *I'm almost starting to believe it myself!*

From Steven's window Elizabeth peered out to the parking lot to see whether any more students were showing up. Besides the lot being absolutely full of cars, she saw a few people gathered in a circle. They were talking and pointing up at the apartment. Elizabeth recognized one of the faces. It was the unmistakably surly face of the man they'd met earlier in the day: Steven's landlord. She pulled back from the window before he noticed her. *Steven's going to kill us!* she thought, beginning to panic.

Elizabeth scanned the room for her sister. It was

hard not to notice Jessica. Her twin was dressed in red and black, dancing with abandon in the middle of the room. She looked as if she didn't have a care in the world. *Why doesn't she ever notice when things get out of control?* Elizabeth wondered angrily. *Will she ever learn when to stop?*

Elizabeth stormed over and grabbed Jessica by the arm. "Jess! We need to talk."

"Can it wait?" Jessica said, wriggling her arm free without losing the beat.

"No. It can't," Elizabeth insisted, standing straight as a rod in the middle of the dance floor. She heard someone mumble, "What's with her?"

"What's up?" Jessica asked lightly, still dancing. Then she added sarcastically, "Are we running out of toilet bowl cleaner?"

Elizabeth grabbed both of Jessica's arms and yanked her out of the dance area. "Stop dancing for a minute and listen to me," Elizabeth said, seething. She ignored the titters and stares around her.

"OK, OK," Jessica said, trying to tug her hands free. Elizabeth guided both of them into the relative quiet of the kitchen before she let go of Jessica's hands.

Jessica rubbed her wrists. "What's so amazingly important that you had to go and embarrass both of us in front of all these people?" she asked.

"This party has to calm down right now," Elizabeth said, "or we're going to have to kick everyone out."

"What?" Jessica gasped. "End the party? You're out of your mind—it's just starting to really rock!"

"That's the problem!" Elizabeth said. "I just saw Steven's landlord talking with a bunch of angry-looking tenants in the parking lot."

"So what?" Jessica asked with a dismissive wave of her hand. "Why should we care about a bunch of boring tenants who have nothing better to do on a Saturday night than complain about a few people having a good time?"

"I'll tell you why we should care, Jess. They called the landlord," Elizabeth told her sister. "If we don't get everyone out, Steven and Billie might come back from their beach vacation to find a big eviction notice plastered on their door."

"Oh, please, Liz," Jessica said, tossing her hair over her shoulder. "You're blowing things way out of proportion. You can't get evicted for having a little party."

"I am not blowing things out of proportion," insisted Elizabeth, her voice rising higher. "First of all, this is not the *little* party you promised. Second of all, didn't you hear Steven tell us about how Oliver got them into hot water with the landlord? This will only make things worse!"

"What do you want me to do about it?" Jessica asked her twin, her hands on her hips. "Tell people to stop having so much fun?"

"Well, for one, you can turn down the stereo and start telling people to find another party somewhere else," Elizabeth said. Just then she saw one of the Thetas step on top of the coffee table and start spinning and dancing to the music.

"She can't dance on there!" Elizabeth fumed. "Jess! Go tell your friend to get off the table right now!"

Jessica turned around to see what had got her sister so upset. But instead of urging the girl off the table, Jessica ran right over and jumped up next to her. The two girls started bumping their hips, bending their knees to dip lower and lower.

"You go girl!" another Theta cried, clapping her hands to the beat. A number of other kids who had been talking or snacking jumped into the dance area. Someone turned up the volume on the stereo.

Elizabeth stood breathless as she watched the party becoming more and more chaotic. If Jessica wasn't going to help her, she would have to take control herself.

She walked over to a group of kids gathered around the snack table. "We've really got to start getting people out of here," Elizabeth said, trying to sound both friendly and serious.

A beautiful girl with straight black hair and crystal-blue eyes asked, "Why?"

"The landlord's going to come knocking any minute," Elizabeth explained.

"Oh, just the landlord? He can't do anything," a redhead said.

"I'm really sorry," Elizabeth tried again, "but I'm going to have to ask you to leave."

"Sure, OK," a chubby guy agreed, as he stuffed a chip piled high with sour-cream dip into his mouth. "Anybody see where I put my beer?"

Elizabeth stood speechless, appalled at their lack of consideration. *No one's going to leave here unless they're put out by force,* she realized. Then she had an idea. If she could just get someone to help her carry out the keg, Elizabeth was sure that the party would follow the beer right out the door.

But as she walked down the hallway to the bathroom, Elizabeth heard the unmistakable sounds of someone retching. A guy was crouched over the toilet bowl, his shoulders heaving with every cough. And to make matters worse, another guy was throwing up right in the bathroom sink. *Gross! That's it,* Elizabeth decided. *I don't care if these people think I'm the biggest geek alive. This party's going to stop right now.*

She headed back to the living room to try another party-ending strategy: stop the music. But there was no way she could push her way through to the stereo. Then she remembered that the whole system was plugged into the wall outlet by the door. In her frenzy to pull the plug on the party, Elizabeth accidentally knocked her hip against a table, sending a cup flying off the edge. She grabbed it before it fell.

She was just reaching down to pull the plug when she heard someone banging on the front door.

Elizabeth froze as she heard a deep and serious male voice on the other side of the door. "Open up!" the voice called. "This is the police!"

Jessica ran up behind her twin. "Don't open the door!" she hissed. "They'll just go away if we quiet down."

"Forget it, Jess," Elizabeth replied curtly. "We can't just ignore the police." The two sisters stood facing one another, staring angrily into each other's eyes. Finally Jessica shrugged her shoulders. If Elizabeth wanted to be stupid enough to answer the door, Jessica wasn't going to stop her. She took a step back and motioned for Elizabeth to open the door.

Elizabeth stepped up and yanked the door open wide. Two uniformed cops stood in the hallway with stern expressions on their faces. The taller one was gripping his baton, bouncing it menacingly in his palm.

"Is there a problem?" Elizabeth asked weakly.

"I'm Sergeant Franklin and this is Sergeant Conneely of the Sweet Valley County Police Department," the shorter cop said. "Who's responsible here?"

"We're responsible," Jessica said, shouldering in front of her sister so that the men could appreciate the full impact of her sexy outfit: a filmy red blouse over a tight black T-shirt and black stretch pants.

The men's faces remained wooden. "We've had a number of complaints from your neighbors about noise levels and the number of cars packed in the parking lot," Sergeant Conneely said.

Jessica gasped, placing a hand flat on her chest. "I'm so sorry. We had no idea we were disturbing anyone," she said in her most innocent voice. "They didn't have to go and trouble you about it. If they had just asked us to turn the stereo down—"

"One lady did," Sergeant Franklin interrupted. "She said some blond girl just laughed in her face and told her to get some earplugs." He glared at the twins.

"Liz! That's so unlike you!" Jessica said, sounding shocked.

Elizabeth glowered and Jessica held her breath, waiting to see how her sister would respond. But before Elizabeth could say anything, the taller cop peered into the cup in Elizabeth's hand and sniffed. "Is that beer you've got there?" he asked.

"Um, I . . . I don't know," Elizabeth said haltingly. "I just picked this up off the table."

"OK. Party's over. Everyone out," he announced, taking a step into the room. Then he looked straight at Elizabeth. "We'll be waiting in the squad car across the street. If you don't have this apartment cleared out in fifteen minutes, we're coming back in with a warrant to check IDs."

Chapter 6

"Do we have any more of that seafood salad?" Steven asked, foraging through the empty plastic take-out containers spread out on the blanket. "It's delicious."

Since they'd had no other romantic options for dinner, Billie had suggested they buy their favorite deli items and bring them to the beach for a nighttime picnic.

"Here it is," Billie said as she handed the container to Steven. "Go ahead and polish it off. I don't think I can eat another bite." She lay back on the blanket and closed her eyes, a peaceful expression on her face.

The night was warm, the stars sparkled in the dark sky, and a gentle breeze floated over the deserted beach. It was a perfect night to rekindle the romance they'd been missing—except for the fact that Steven couldn't get Elizabeth and Jessica out of his mind.

Walking through the sleepy town earlier with Billie, Steven had wondered how his sisters had spent their afternoon. Even though the twins thought of themselves as worldly, they were only juniors in high school, after all. Steven thought back to his own experience visiting colleges and remembered how intimidating the whole thing had seemed. *Were Jess and Liz able to figure out something fun to do with their Saturday night?* he worried.

A pitiful picture formed in his mind: the twins sitting side by side on his lumpy couch, channel-surfing through the measly selections on Saturday-night television. *I'm their big brother,* he thought. *I should be there showing them a good time.*

Then he took the thought a step further. What if he and Billie had canceled their plans and stayed home with the twins? Steven knew how fortunate he was to have a girlfriend who was so understanding about Oliver's disastrous visit. After everything she'd endured, the last thing Billie deserved was to have yet another set of Steven's houseguests infringe upon her life.

Besides, the twins were resourceful, Steven convinced himself. Elizabeth and Jessica could take care of themselves. He looked over at Billie lying prone on the blanket, eyes closed, a satisfied smile on her face. She looked so beautiful, so happy. Billie really needed this weekend. *We both* need *this weekend,*

Steven thought peacefully. *To be together.*

"This was a great idea, Billie," Steven said as he gathered plastic utensils, paper napkins, and food wrappers into one garbage bag.

"Thanks, Steven. But it was more like a last resort," Billie said wryly. "It was either this or fried grease for dinner."

"No—I don't just mean the picnic," he explained. "I mean the whole trip. Finding this place and planning a weekend getaway for us. Now that we're away from everything, I'm realizing how much I've missed *us*. Just you and me alone together."

"Oh, Steven, I've missed it, too," Billie said, rolling onto her side and raising herself on one elbow. "Now, come down here and give your girlfriend a proper kiss."

"Yes, ma'am. Right away." Steven lowered his body onto the blanket, kissing Billie firmly on the mouth. After a minute he pulled his head back and ran his hand lightly over her cheek.

"You're so beautiful, Billie," he said. "I don't know what I did to deserve you."

"You don't have to do anything to deserve me," Billie whispered. "I love you, Steven Wakefield."

"I love you, too," Steven said hoarsely, his voice catching. He gazed intently into Billie's face, noticing a faint glimmer of gold in the brown of her eyes—a reflection of the candle flickering beside her. The sight filled him with an overwhelming sense of well-being. He felt a lump form in his throat, and he closed his eyes and buried his face in Billie's neck.

"Hey! That tickles," she said, giggling. She pushed him off her and looked into his face. "Steven, are you crying?" she asked, her brows gathering with concern.

Steven wiped at his eyes. "No," he explained quietly. "I think I just got some sand—"

"Don't give me that, Steven Wakefield," Billie said in a scolding tone. "I know the difference between watery eyes and tears. Why are you crying?"

Steven grinned with embarrassment. "I'm happy, Billie," he told her. "They're tears of joy. Pretty sappy, huh?"

"Pretty wonderful," Billie corrected him, her own eyes welling up with tears.

"OK, enough of this sentimental stuff," Steven said with mock gruffness. "Or next thing we know, a trio of violinists will appear from the night sky to serenade us."

Billie glanced up at the sky. "Well, maybe not violins," she said, sounding worried. "But there *are* a bunch of clouds up there that weren't there before. We should probably go in. It looks like rain."

"Thanks for coming! Sorry for the trouble!" Jessica called after the departing guests. "Hope to see you again soon!"

Elizabeth shook her head. How could Jessica be so light and friendly at a time like this? The apartment was a mess, the cops were still sitting in their car right across the street, and there was a half-full keg of beer in the bathroom. *At least the party's over,* Elizabeth thought with relief. And with any luck, the cops would be satisfied when they saw everyone leaving.

Elizabeth went to the window to check on the cops just in time to see their squad car's headlights turn on. The cop in the driver's seat looked up at the window and gave Elizabeth a quick wave. Then the policemen pulled out of the parking spot and drove away.

Whew, Elizabeth thought. *I'm glad that's over.* Now she had only the considerable task of figuring out what to do with the keg. She walked down the hall toward the bathroom and was startled to see someone sitting on the edge of Steven and Billie's bed, engrossed in a book.

"Party's over, time to go home," she said with a half-smile, barely hiding her exasperation. The guy looked up with a quick jerk of his head. When he saw Elizabeth, he jumped to his feet, inadvertently letting the book in his lap drop to the floor. As he bent over to pick it up, his glasses slid off his face.

"Is everyone gone?" he asked as he fumbled under the bed to retrieve his glasses.

"Everyone except you," Elizabeth answered, holding back a giggle.

"I'm so sorry, I had no idea," he said. He located his glasses, pushed them onto his face, and then swiped a lock of brown hair out of his eyes. "I don't know what came over me," he said apologetically, biting his lower lip. "I was just—"

"It's OK, really," Elizabeth interrupted with a friendly smile before he got too carried away with his apologies. Despite her earlier exasperation, Elizabeth found herself charmed by his sincere show of embarrassment. The guy was really cute, with unkempt curly brown hair, fair skin, and bright-red lips. "What book had you so engrossed that you didn't even hear the commotion out here?" she asked him.

"I hope you don't mind, but I had been really meaning to get this book, and when I saw it sitting on the desk here, I couldn't help myself. I'm really sorry," he said, holding the book up for Elizabeth to see. It was a book she had brought with her, a new biography she was reading about Edward R. Murrow, one of the pioneers of television news.

"Oh! I love that book," she said.

"I do, too!" he said with enthusiasm. "I mean, I love Edward R. Murrow, and I like the little I've read of this book so far."

Elizabeth laughed. "My name's Elizabeth," she said, holding out her hand.

"Ian, Ian Cooke," he said, switching the book to his left arm so he could take her hand. "Good to meet you."

"Are you into journalism?" Elizabeth asked.

"I guess you could say that," Ian said with a grin. "I've sure spent a lot of time doing it. I was editor of my high-school paper, I've written articles for the community paper, and I'm a journalism major."

"Wow," Elizabeth said. "That's an impressive résumé."

"Hardly," Ian said modestly. "And yourself? You must be a journalism buff if you find this kind of thing interesting." He nodded at the book in his hand.

"Well, there's the column for my high-school paper, articles for the community paper, and plans to be a journalism major," she said. They both laughed.

"I guess we have a lot in common," Ian said.

"I guess so," Elizabeth whispered. They stood for a minute, their eyes locked. *Is it me, or is there some chemistry going on here?* Elizabeth wondered. Then she rejected the feeling. *What am I thinking? My love for Todd is so strong, I couldn't possibly be interested in anyone else.*

"Are you taking any journalism classes now?" Ian asked.

"No, I—"

"No? Well, then you'll just have to come sit in on the advanced class I'm taking. It's being taught by Felicia Newkirk. She's a—"

"Felicia Newkirk?" Elizabeth asked excitedly. "*The* Felicia Newkirk?"

Ian smiled. "You've heard of her, then."

"Of course I have! Felicia Newkirk was the first woman to break into the male-dominated White House press corps. I practically went into mourning when she retired from the profession," Elizabeth said, pulling out a chair by the desk to sit down. "I had no idea she became a professor."

"She's not really a professor—she's not affiliated with a university," Ian explained. "She just travels around, doing a semester here, a semester there."

"Wow, what a life," Elizabeth gushed. "She must have more stories . . ."

"She's been sharing some real interesting stuff about the Kennedy administration," Ian said with a chuckle. "So what do you say, do you want to come sit in on a class? It's a small seminar, but I'm sure she won't mind."

"I'd love to!" Elizabeth said enthusiastically.

"Great," he said. "Well, I guess I'd better be going." He stood up and began walking down the hallway toward the front door as she followed. He let his eyes stray over the mess in the living room. "Unless you need some help cleaning up," he offered.

"Thank you," Elizabeth said with a tired smile. "That's really nice of you to offer, but I think we can manage."

"You sure?" he asked. "This looks like a disaster zone."

"We'll be fine. It looks worse than it really is," Elizabeth said, wishing she could believe her own words.

After Ian had left, Elizabeth thought, *What a nice guy. Most guys wouldn't even notice the mess, let alone offer to help clean up.* Then she smiled and hugged her arms tight around herself. There was one other guy who would insist on helping: Todd. Although Ian was cute, he couldn't hold a candle to the wonderful relationship she shared with Todd. *I just hope Ian's not interested in me,* Elizabeth thought.

Zach had stayed with Jessica to help her make sure everyone left safely, and to help her deal with the cops if they returned. Now, with the guests and the police gone, Jessica was sitting on the kitchen counter, her legs dangling in front of the dishwasher. She looked at Zach leaning against the sink, imagining the story she would report to her best friend, Lila Fowler.

Lila, you would have died, Jessica imagined telling her friend. *Me, Jessica Wakefield, high-school junior, threw one of the best parties Sweet Valley U has ever seen. Everybody who was anybody was there from the best sororities and fraternities on campus. And I met the cutest premed student of all time: Zachary Marsden.*

But Zach was more than just cute. He was thoughtful and kind. It was as if he didn't even know how cute he was, or what a great catch he was. Jessica felt a burst of happiness from deep within her that was so overwhelming, she let out a little shiver.

"Are you cold?" Zach asked with concern.

"No, just happy," Jessica said. "I'm really glad you came to the party. I've really enjoyed talking to you."

"I feel the same way," Zach said, looking deep

into her eyes. Then he shyly glanced down at his feet.

He's as crazy about me as I am about him, Jessica realized.

"I wanted to ask you something," Zach said, leaning over to peek through the open kitchen door. "Is that other gorgeous blond girl your sister?"

"Elizabeth?" Jessica asked, confused.

"Is that her name?" Zach asked. "Anyway, I thought for sure you must be twins, but I overheard her talking about being in high school."

Jessica almost choked on her soda. "Oh, right. Well, actually, she's my younger sister."

"Wow," Zach said. "You look absolutely identical."

"I know, isn't it amazing?" Jessica replied with a casual laugh. "You'd never believe how many people think we're twins."

"It's eerie," Zach said, shaking his head in amazement. *Unbelievable is more like it,* Jessica chuckled to herself. *That was a close one.*

"So what can I tell you about California?" she asked quickly, to change the subject.

Zach narrowed his eyes and stared into the space over her head. "Hmm, let's see," he said, rubbing his chin. "Oh—I know!" He grinned mischievously at Jessica.

"What?" she asked, returning the grin.

"Why is it that all you California girls think that guys from the East Coast are uptight and boring?"

"Maybe because you are?" Jessica teased.

"Oh, great, thanks a lot," Zach said, pretending to

be hurt. "So I guess you were just humoring me when you said how glad you were to have met me."

Jessica gave him a warm smile. "No, I'm just kidding. I really am glad I met you," she said with affection. Their eyes remained locked together for what felt like an eternity. Jessica's heart was beating so hard, she could feel her ears tingle as they filled up with blood.

"What else can I tell you about California?" she asked sweetly.

"OK," he began. "Why is it that everyone in California drives with their top down all the time, even when it's really cold outside?"

"It's never so cold in California that you want to drive around all cooped up with a roof over your head," Jessica replied. "Besides, you can always turn on the heat!"

Zach laughed. "You mean you actually turn on the heat instead of putting up the top?"

"Sure, why not?" Jessica replied.

"I take it you drive a convertible," he said, his eyes crinkled with laughter.

"Actually, it's a Jeep," she said.

"I love Jeeps!" Zach said, his eyes sparkling. "I've always wanted to drive one." He looked at her expectantly.

"Well, I can see about arranging for a test drive," Jessica said, forming a wonderful picture in her mind. The wind whipping through her hair, and Zach in the driver's seat, dressed in a loose T-shirt and shorts. She was suddenly overcome with the urge to make that picture a reality.

"When can I see you again?" Zach asked suddenly.

Jessica's mind went blank. It was one thing to be flirting with a guy at a party, another thing to actually make plans to see him again. That would be a date. And she had a boyfriend. It would be wrong of her to start something with Zach when Ken was waiting patiently at home.

Then she looked into Zach's green eyes, noticing for the first time that they were speckled with gold. She felt her resolve melt. *What's the real harm in seeing him again?* she wondered. *It's not like I'm going to actually get involved with Zach—I'm only here for a week. It's harmless,* she decided.

"How about tomorrow night?" Jessica asked.

"Great!"

Elizabeth suddenly appeared in the doorway. "Jessica!" she snapped. "The party's over and the place is a mess. What are you doing still sitting here yapping?"

Jessica glared at her sister with annoyance. Couldn't Elizabeth see that she was ruining a perfect moment? "Do you think you could give us a min—"

"No, it's OK," Zach broke in. "I was just leaving. See you tomorrow?" he asked, looking at Jessica.

"I can't wait," she purred.

"I just can't believe how much you two look alike," Zach said to Elizabeth as he walked past her. "I could have sworn you were iden—"

"I'll walk you to the door," Jessica blurted, jumping off the counter. She didn't want Elizabeth to figure out that she had lied to Zach about being her older sister. Elizabeth just wouldn't understand. And the last thing Jessica needed was to have her twin sister crash her postparty high with a lecture.

Zach gave Jessica the lightest of kisses at the door, leaving her lips tingling for more. She closed the door and swooned. "What a great party!" she exclaimed out loud, flopping onto the couch. She felt the crunch of potato chips underneath her.

Elizabeth walked out from the bathroom, bucket and mop in hand, and was annoyed to find Jessica slumped on the couch looking dreamily at the ceiling.

"You get bathroom duty," Elizabeth declared. "Maybe that'll help you understand why it was such a stupid idea to have a keg. Did you happen to notice the two guys puking?"

"Gross!" Jessica exclaimed. "How can people be such pigs?" She crossed her arms and shook her head.

"Would you just hurry up and help me?" Elizabeth said with a sigh. "This place is a wreck, and we have to get everything back the way it was, or Steven will have both our heads." She looked around the living room. There were beer cans and plastic cups on every surface, most of them partially filled with liquid—some with cigarette butts floating in them. CDs were scattered about the room, and a few were sitting under beer cans like coasters. Billie's art posters were hanging off the walls. Someone had stacked empty beer bottles underneath the coffee table, and potato chips and dip were mushed all over the carpet.

What made me think we could get away with this? Elizabeth wondered morosely. *Why don't I ever learn that Jessica's ideas almost always end in disaster?*

Elizabeth set to work picking up cups and beer cans. She gasped in horror when she found cigarette butts in the pot of the new ficus tree. "Is nothing sacred?" she said out loud.

Elizabeth's blood pressure rose as she realized the enormity of the task ahead of her. And Jessica was still sitting as if paralyzed on the couch.

"Jessica!" Elizabeth snapped. "This place is not going to clean itself!"

"I'm so tired, Liz," Jessica said with an exaggerated sigh. "And sitting here watching you running around like a chicken with its head cut off is making me even more tired."

"And what do you suggest we do?" Elizabeth demanded. "Set the whole place on fire and tell Steven and Billie there was a gas leak?"

"That's not a bad idea. . . ." Jessica mused, her hand stroking her chin.

Elizabeth was aghast. "Jess!" she exclaimed.

"I was only kidding, Liz," Jessica said with a sigh.

"I just think that as tired as we are, it'll be a waste of time for us to try to clean tonight. We should just get some sleep and deal with the mess tomorrow."

Elizabeth realized that her sister had a point. She'd been cleaning like crazy for the last few minutes, and there wasn't even a small dent in the mess. *Maybe after a good night's sleep, we'll be able to tackle the job systematically,* Elizabeth thought.

"OK, you win," Elizabeth relented, wanting nothing more than to fall into a deep, dreamless sleep. "But you still get bathroom duties tomorrow."

"Right," Jessica agreed, dragging herself off the couch. "I'll take the bedroom," she said, and she disappeared behind the closed door before Elizabeth could say anything.

"I guess that means I get the couch," Elizabeth grumbled to herself.

After setting up the fold-out bed, Elizabeth crawled under the covers and looked around the apartment one last time before she turned off the light. *It won't look nearly as bad in the light of day,* she tried to convince herself, pushing away the pit of worry that had lodged in her stomach. *We'll just have to get the place spotless before Steven and Billie come home.*

Drifting off to sleep, Elizabeth tried to remember when Billie had said they'd be back.

Chapter 7

Steven fixed his eyes on the crack above him as he watched the yellow light from the street corner wash rhythmically across the ceiling. *Have I gotten any sleep at all tonight?* he wondered.

Every time he moved, it seemed another loose spring stabbed him in a new place. He had finally settled on a corpselike position, lying flat on his back, his arms crossed over his chest.

What did I do to deserve this? he thought morosely. *Now I know why this place was so dirt cheap, why no guidebooks mention this town, and why the parking lot was so empty when we got here.* He turned his head to look out the window. The sky was still dark—very dark. *Is morning ever going to come?*

Steven must have drifted off, because the next thing he knew, he was jerked awake by the sound of clapping over his head. He looked at the ceiling, realizing that the clouds, heavy with rain all evening, had finally broken. It was pouring.

The thin roof didn't muffle the sound. This was no light pitter-patter; this was a loud and heavy drumbeat, filling Steven's head with noise. And then he felt something cold hit his face. *The roof is leaking!* he realized with a shiver. Raindrops fell onto his forehead, in his eye, dribbling cold water down his cheeks. *I know I didn't do anything to deserve this,* he thought miserably.

He knew he had to get out of that inn, or he'd lose his mind. Steven looked over to where Billie was sleeping on the bed. "Billie!" he whispered, figuring she couldn't possibly be sleeping through the noise. "Billie!" he whispered a little more loudly. She didn't respond. Through the darkness Steven could see that she was lying curled up on her side, her back facing him, peaceful and still. *I can't believe she's actually able to sleep,* Steven thought, watching her dark figure rise and fall with every breath.

Should he wake her up? *No,* he decided after a minute. *At least one of us should get a good night's sleep. Besides, Billie doesn't need to know how miserable I am. She's been beating herself up enough about this place as it is.*

Resigned to spending a sleepless night, Steven groaned and rolled over carefully to avoid being jabbed by another loose spring, and he folded his arm over his head to shield himself from the drips. The stench of mildew wafted up from the couch.

All of a sudden Billie cried, "This is ridiculous!" She bolted upright and flicked on the light switch next to the bed.

"You're awake!" Steven exclaimed, rubbing his eyes as the room filled with light.

"Of course I'm awake," Billie moaned, her hands clenched into fists. "I've got about four different puddles forming in the dents in my mattress, and my pillow is nothing but a hard, flat cotton brick," she said, looking plaintively at Steven through bloodshot eyes.

She let out a small sob. "And the sound of the wind whistling through the cracks keeps making me dream I'm eight years old again, suffering through endless violin lessons," she wailed. "I can't remember ever being more miserable."

As tears started streaming down Billie's face, Steven felt his heart swell with sympathy. He jumped up and went to the bed, pulling her into his arms. Billie sobbed into Steven's chest. "I've barely even slept at all," she said softly.

"You haven't either?" Steven asked, chuckling warmly. "I don't think I've slept more than a few minutes all night." He stroked her hair.

Billie pulled herself away to look at Steven. Then she bit her lip and looked down.

"What is it, Billie?" Steven prompted her.

Billie took a deep breath and bit her lip again. "Do you think it would be ridiculous for us to drive home tonight?" she asked in a small voice.

"I thought you'd never ask," Steven sighed with

relief. "That's just fine with me. Let's clear out of here."

"Oh, good," Billie said, an expression of happiness washing over her face.

"The way I look at it," Steven said, reaching down to the floor for his socks, "we gave this our best shot—we really tried to make it work. But we just have to cut our losses and face the fact that our weekend getaway at the beach was not meant to be." He pulled on a sock.

"Oh, Steven—" Billie began.

"And don't you start in on your apologies, Billie Winkler," Steven interrupted, pointing a finger at her. "Because I refuse to listen to any more of your blaming yourself for the way this weekend turned out. It was a great idea and I was all for it. Besides, let's face it—neither of us could have possibly imagined how horrible this place would turn out to be." He laughed, and after a moment Billie joined in.

"Thanks, Steven," she said. "Thanks for being so understanding." She hugged him tightly, until they felt more drips falling from the ceiling. "Let's make a run for it!" she cried. "Before the roof caves in!"

They gathered their things quickly, giggling every time they tiptoed onto another creak in the old wooden floor. They were packed and ready in less than ten minutes.

"Look on the bright side," Steven said in the car, after he had relished the sound of the engine turning over. "At least now we'll get back in time to take the twins out for a great breakfast."

Elizabeth's eyes fluttered open at the sound of a key turning in the lock. Was it a robber? A crazy ax murderer? *Steven?*

The previous night came rushing back to Elizabeth in a flurry. *Oh, no!* she thought desperately. *The apartment's a total disaster!* Elizabeth had seen Steven fly off the handle before, and it was not a pleasant sight. She almost hoped that it *was* a robber on the other side of the door.

From where she was lying on the sofa bed, Elizabeth had a clear view of the door. She clutched the comforter tightly around her, watching with dread as Steven and Billie walked in, giggling. Even in the dim light of early morning, she could see the expressions on their faces turn from smiles to shock.

"What the—" Steven yelled, punching on the light switch. "What happened here?" he raged when he saw the room fully illuminated.

Elizabeth jumped out of bed and grabbed the jeans she had left crumpled on the floor. "I'm so sorry you had to come home to see your place looking like this," Elizabeth said apologetically as she tugged on her jeans. "We were too tired to clean last night, so we were going to wake up bright and early to get everything clean today!"

Steven glared at her. "That's supposed to make me feel better? You're telling me that you were planning to hide all the evidence so that I would never find out you used our apartment for a party free-for-all?"

Elizabeth stood speechless, her eyes filling with tears.

"We leave you alone for one night, and this is what happens!" Steven continued to rail. "And to think I actually felt bad last night about leaving you by yourselves!"

Billie didn't say a word but quietly began to pick up glasses and plates while Steven stalked around the apartment. He kicked an empty potato-chip bag. "Have you lost every ounce of consideration and respect?"

Elizabeth sucked in her breath, finding no words with which to defend herself. Steven was right. There was no excuse, no explanation, no defense for paying back Steven and Billie's generosity by acting so irresponsibly and carelessly. *If only I hadn't listened to Jessica last night,* Elizabeth admonished herself. *Even a whole army wouldn't have been able to get this place cleaned up in one day, but at least Billie and Steven wouldn't have come home to a complete disaster area.*

"Can't I get some sleep around here?" Jessica's sleepy voice called out from the bedroom. She walked into the living room, rubbing her eyes. "What's all the yelling about?"

Then she stopped in her tracks. "Steven! Billie! You're home!"

"Damn right we're home!" Steven bellowed. His face, which had been getting redder by the minute, was now crimson. His eyes bulged in their sockets, looking as if they would pop out any minute. "You'd better have a really good explanation for this, young lady." He crossed his arms in front of him, his mouth set in a tight line.

Jessica stood dumbfounded for a minute. Then Elizabeth saw her eyes dart about, the telltale sign of the devious mind of Jessica Wakefield at work. Elizabeth was curious to hear the excuse her sister would invent this time.

Jessica's face took on a serious expression. "I know this looks really bad, but there's a perfectly reasonable explanation—"

"Which is?" Steven put his hands on his hips.

"If you'd just let me finish my sentence, Steven, I'd be perfectly happy to explain." Jessica stared at her brother as if he were the one in trouble. "You see, Liz and I went to the dorms yesterday and started talking to some cool students. We would have stayed there talking all night, but—" She stopped. "But the dorms were being fumigated for pests. There seems to be a huge mouse problem . . . and everyone had to leave their rooms," she explained reasonably.

"So you invited the whole dorm back to your brother's apartment?" Steven demanded, staring goggle-eyed at his younger sister.

"No," Jessica said, shaking her head. "We just invited a few people. How were we to know that there was absolutely nothing else interesting to do on this entire campus last night? Everybody ended up coming to our little get-together—they crashed. Right, Liz?" Jessica looked at her twin with pleading eyes.

Elizabeth didn't know what to say. Even though she felt somewhat responsible, this really was mostly Jessica's fault. But Elizabeth knew that if she told Steven what had really happened, he would never trust either of them again.

"Jess is right, Steven," Elizabeth said, resigned to the small lie. "We had no idea how fast word spreads about parties. We only invited a few people over, and before we knew it, the apartment was full. But we kicked everyone out before anything really bad happened." *Except for the fact that the police showed up*, a voice inside Elizabeth's head reminded her.

Watching the vein throb in Steven's neck, Elizabeth decided to wait until his blood pressure dropped before telling him about the visit from the police. Or about the keg in the bathroom.

How do I let myself get into such messes? she thought woefully. She looked over at her sister, who was standing in her rumpled nightgown, an anxious expression on her face. *You owe me, Jessica Wakefield. Big-time.*

Steven looked at his sisters' nervous faces. "You'd better start packing," he said. "Because I'm going to call Mom and Dad right now and tell them what you've done. I can't wait to hear what kind of punishment they dream up when they find out you wrecked my apartment on your first night here," he added, walking over to the telephone.

"Please don't call them, Steven," Elizabeth begged.

"Give me one good reason why I shouldn't," Steven retorted. His fingers hovered over the dialing pad.

"Well, for one thing," Jessica said, her tone light, "I don't think they'd be too happy to hear that our older brother left his underage sisters all alone on their first night away from home." Jessica smiled at her brother, her eyebrows raised in a smug arch.

Steven, bristling with annoyance, put down the receiver. He hated to admit it, but Jessica had a point. He'd probably get into just as much trouble as the twins. He had no choice but to keep his outrage a secret.

"All right, you win," he relented. "But if you think Billie and I are going to help you clean up this mess, you're dead wrong." He walked down the hall to the bedroom, slamming the door behind him.

A few minutes later Steven was stewing on the bed when he heard a soft knock. "Steven?" Billie's voice called through the door. "Can I talk to you for a minute?"

"Of course," he grunted.

Billie opened the door. "Please don't bite my head off, but I think we should help clean up," she said quietly.

"No way," Steven retorted. "Why should we have

to clean up their mess? I know you can't help yourself from being nice, but Jess and Liz dug their own graves. They'll just have to dig themselves out of it."

"It's not about being nice, Steven," Billie maintained. "I just don't want to have to sleep in this filth, and the more people that pitch in, the faster this place will be back to normal."

Steven reluctantly agreed, and the four of them spent all day Sunday cleaning up the apartment. Not much was said, except for Steven's occasional outbursts. "Why did I ever agree to let the two of you visit?" he moaned when he discovered the keg in the shower.

Even Billie snapped when she unearthed her favorite silk robe in a tangled ball behind the toilet. "Don't these people have any respect for privacy?" she wailed.

Finally, with four garbage bags stuffed full to bursting, and the keg loaded in the back of Steven's car to be returned to the liquor store in the morning, Steven called it quits.

"I'm taking a nap, so you'd better be quiet," he announced. Shutting the bedroom door behind him, Steven lay down on the bed, hoping to make up for the sleep he'd missed the night before. But it was no use. He was too angry to sleep. He decided he might as well get some studying done.

But that didn't work either. His concentration was so shot, he read the same paragraph over about four times before Billie opened the door, a platter of nachos in her arms.

"I didn't think you'd be able to sleep," she said. "So I made us a snack."

Steven broke into a smile. He hadn't eaten all day. "At least one good thing came from the party: left-overs!"

"Never underestimate the power of cheese to soothe the savage beast," Billie joked as Steven stuffed a big handful of chips, cheese, and salsa into his mouth. He laughed, feeling his dour mood lift.

After they had eaten the plate clean, Steven took Billie's hand. "If I had known the twins would be such a nuisance, I never would have agreed to let them stay here," he said. "Especially after Oliver."

"They're just kids having fun," Billie said agreeably. "Outside of the fact that our curtains now reek of cigarette smoke once again, it doesn't look like there's any lasting damage. Besides, the day will come when this episode will be something we can laugh about."

"Maybe in twenty years," Steven said with a wry laugh. "You're really great, Billie. I owe you."

"No, you don't owe me," Billie said, shaking her head. "But, actually, there is one thing you could do for me."

"Name it."

"Never say the name 'Oliver' again. Every time I hear it, I get nauseated," Billie said, holding her stomach.

Steven shook Billie's hand. "Deal."

Just then Elizabeth appeared in the bedroom

doorway, a guilty expression on her face. "Steven, your landlord's at the door," she said with a grimace.

"Oh, great," groaned Steven, bracing himself for another lecture from his persnickety landlord.

After a full five-minute tirade about the despicable display of inconsiderate behavior the night before, Mr. Delp took a breath, giving Steven his first opportunity to apologize. "We're all very sorry about this," Steven said.

"You'd better be sorry," the landlord replied. "One more party like that, and I'll have you out of here so fast, you won't have time to pack your toothbrush."

"It will never happen again," Steven promised.

"You're telling me it won't. No more parties—nothing. If you have more than six people in this place at one time, you'd better make sure you clear it with me first," Mr. Delp warned. He turned and marched off.

After Mr. Delp's tense figure disappeared down the hall, Steven looked at the twins sitting side by side on the couch. "You'd just better be the world's best guests for the rest of the week," Steven said menacingly.

Later that evening Jessica lay on the couch, squeezing her temples between her fingers. So far Steven had just threatened to send the twins home. But Jessica knew that if he discovered she was going out on a date tonight with a college student, and that she was pretending to be in college herself, he definitely would send them packing. So Jessica was using the oldest excuse in the book: the headache.

"Are you sure you don't want to come with us?" Billie asked for the sixth time. "I hate to leave you here all by yourself."

"Thanks, Billie, but I think I just need to let this headache run its course," Jessica explained for what she hoped was the last time. "Don't worry about me, I'll be fine." *I'd be much better if you guys would hurry up and leave,* she added to herself. Zach was due at seven o'clock, and it was nearly half past six. And she still had to change.

"Leave her, Billie," Steven grumbled. "If Jessica wants to stay home and pout all night, that's her problem." Then he gave his sister a warning glare. "As long as she isn't planning on inviting anyone over."

"Don't be ridiculous, Steven. My head is killing me—the last thing I want to do is be social." Actually, the last thing Jessica wanted to do was go with Elizabeth, Billie, and Steven to a philosophy lecture at the student union that night. And being social was the first thing Jessica wanted to do. Being social with Zach Marsden, that is. She just had to make sure she got home before they did.

"What time did you say you'd be back?" she asked casually.

"Why?" Elizabeth inquired, narrowing her eyes with suspicion.

"I just wanted to know whether I have time to

take a long nap," Jessica replied. "Otherwise, I'll just stay awake until you get home."

"We could hang out for a while after the lecture so that you can have a long stretch of peace and quiet," Billie suggested.

"Oh, that's so sweet of you, Billie," Jessica cooed, calculating how much time that would give her with Zach. Elizabeth and Steven looked grumpy, but neither of them argued.

Finally, after torturous dawdling, they put on their coats. Walking past Jessica's prone figure on the couch, Elizabeth glared down at her. "Don't ruin this for me," Elizabeth hissed. Jessica met her eye and smiled. Elizabeth knew Jessica as only a twin could—and she obviously knew the headache was an act. But Jessica also knew Elizabeth wouldn't give her sister away.

As soon as she heard the door shut behind them, Jessica leaped up from the couch and ran to the bedroom to change. Within minutes she had stripped out of her jeans and SVU sweatshirt and was dressed in her new golden-brown chenille turtleneck sweater over black leggings and boots.

Jessica appraised her outfit in the full-length mirror that hung on the closet door. The sweater was definitely a positive addition to her wardrobe, she decided. She hadn't been sure when she'd bought it—its color was in the beige family, and Jessica usually went for bolder styles. But this shade brought out the golden highlights in her hair.

This college adventure was turning out to be better than she could have hoped. Not only was she going on a date with a college man, tomorrow she had a date for tea at Theta House. And lots of new friends.

She knew she had made a good first impression with the Thetas. Even though the cops had cut the party short, all the Theta girls had congratulated her on a party well-done as they'd walked out the door. *If this is what college is going to be like, I can't wait!* she thought happily.

She was just finishing dabbing her lips with color when the doorbell rang. Jessica's stomach was full of butterflies until she caught sight of herself in the hall mirror on the way to answer the door. She smiled. "Do I even need to ask who's the fairest of them all?" she whispered out loud to her reflection. Then, giddy with excitement, she ran to let in Zach.

Chapter 8

After the lecture Elizabeth, Billie, and Steven went to the Coffee House, a popular SVU hangout. Elizabeth insisted on treating, figuring it was the least she could do. "Go ahead—get anything you want," Elizabeth offered. "It's on me."

"Thanks, Liz," Billie said. She turned to the woman standing behind the bakery counter. "I think I'll go for one of those tasty-looking slices of carrot cake with my double latte," she said.

Steven went on a search for a free table while Billie and Elizabeth loaded up on napkins and utensils. He motioned for them to join him at a table where two girls were just in the process of leaving. The girls hadn't even finished putting their books and papers into their bags.

"Is it always such a fight for a table?" Elizabeth asked after the girls had gone and they were settled in their seats.

"Things get pretty hairy here, especially on Sunday nights," Billie said. "That's the time when everyone who has been procrastinating all weekend gets stressed about all the work they still have to do. It's a big study night," she explained.

"Does anybody actually get any studying done here?" Elizabeth asked. She couldn't imagine studying in a place like this. The tiny tables were crammed close together, and loud jazz music bounced off the brick walls dotted with posters and student artwork. Most of the people looked as if they were too busy talking and scoping out members of the opposite sex to notice the books lying open in front of them.

"It's more peaceful than the dorms," Billie said, laughing wryly.

"Why don't they go to the library?" Elizabeth asked.

"Maybe they're just more into socializing and having a good time than being mature," Steven said cynically. He slurped at his cappuccino.

Elizabeth could see that Steven's mood had not improved in the past two hours. She couldn't help but think that the lecture on the decline of ethics in modern-day society had not done anything to improve her stature in Steven's eyes.

"Steven, please believe me when I tell you how sorry I am about the party last night," Elizabeth said apologetically.

Steven grunted in response.

"We never would have invited those students over

if we had known it would get so big," she tried again.

"But you didn't even ask permission to have *any-one* over!" Steven said with an exasperated sigh.

"I know." Elizabeth twisted the napkin in her lap more tightly. "I don't know what came over me. I guess I was just so excited about being at college that I didn't think."

"You can say that again," Steven snarled. He tried another sip of his cappuccino and took a bite of his brownie, purposefully avoiding her eyes.

It looks like I'll never live this one down, Elizabeth thought grimly.

Billie patted Elizabeth's hand. "Give him time to brood," she said soothingly. "He'll get over it. The best thing to do is ignore him." Steven shot Billie a glare.

"Don't give me that look, Steven Wakefield," Billie said, pointing a finger at Steven's glowering face. "I know how stubborn you can get. Can't you see Elizabeth feels bad enough? I mean, it's not like you've never done anything stupid."

Steven grunted again, folding his arms across his chest.

Thank you, Elizabeth mouthed to Billie.

Billie laughed suddenly, as if struck by a memory. "Once I went to visit my older sister at college, and I pulled the most amazing stunt," Billie said. "Wait until you hear this, Liz." Billie went on to describe how her sister had left her alone in her dorm room one evening. Feeling intellectual and sophisticated,

Billie had lit a bunch of candles and sat down at her sister's computer to write the great American novel.

Unfortunately, within minutes she had managed to lose all of her sister's notes for a big research paper. Then, when Billie had gone in search of a computer expert to help retrieve the files off the hard drive, she had accidentally locked herself out of the room.

"I had just got the RA to open the door when I heard a cacophony of bells and buzzers—a fire alarm. The whole building had to be evacuated until they figured out the source." Billie paused and Steven started giggling.

"I'm guessing that you had something to do with it," Elizabeth said with a smile.

Billie nodded. "I had put one of the candles directly under the fire alarm's heat sensor."

Elizabeth burst out laughing. Steven, who had been holding himself back, joined her laughter.

"OK, you guys," Billie said after a minute. "That's enough. It's not *that* funny."

"I'm sorry, it really isn't," Elizabeth replied, her eyes tearing. "So were you able to retrieve the computer files?"

"Oh! That's the best part!" Billie said. "I hadn't deleted the files at all—I had just put them in a different directory by mistake."

"I can't believe your sister ever let you live that one down," Steven said, laughing. Elizabeth laughed, too, partly because it was a funny story, but mostly out of relief that after a full day of scowls, Steven had finally broken a smile.

"This looks like the hottest spot in town," Jessica said, taking a seat at one of the only available tables in the restaurant. "What's it called again?"

"Jo-Jo's," Zach answered. "It only opened a couple months ago, but it's the first juice bar around campus."

Jessica nodded. "Oh, that makes sense," she said knowingly, even though she'd never been to a juice bar. She looked over the menu. Guava juice? Soba noodles? Somehow she had the feeling they didn't serve milk shakes and fries—her snacks of choice at her favorite restaurant hangout, the Dairi Burger.

"What can I get you?" a bored female voice asked.

Jessica looked up to see a pale face punctuated by a splash of red lipstick and two fine slivers where eyebrows should have been. The waitress was dressed all in black, her shirt and vest hanging loosely over a long cotton skirt. The look was finished with a pair of Doc Martens.

"I'll have whatever he's having," Jessica said weakly, wishing she had worn more black.

"We'll just take two vegetable zingers, please," Zach said, handing both of their menus to the waitress.

A few minutes later the pale-faced girl came back with two glasses of murky brown liquid. Jessica eyed the beverages with unconcealed distaste.

"I know it looks nasty, but give it a try," Zach prompted. "You just might like it."

"I'm sure it tastes great," Jessica said agreeably, taking a small sip of her juice. It tasted like motor oil—or what she imagined motor oil would taste like. She tried not to wince too obviously.

Zach laughed. "It's OK. You don't have to pretend to like it. I guess you could call vegetable juice an *acquired* taste." He took a sip of his juice and smacked his lips as if to prove his point. "I've never been a big fan of vegetables, but when you juice them, one glass keeps the motor running smoothly all day."

Jessica laughed to herself at Zach's choice of metaphors. *I guess I wasn't too far off with the motor-oil comparison.*

"So that's why I hear you purring," she said out loud, blushing immediately at her boldness.

"Is it getting hot in here?" Zach asked, tugging at the collar of his polo shirt. "Or is it just me?" He was blushing, too.

Their flirtation was interrupted by some commotion at the door.

"Give it back!" someone shouted. A group of young teens had come in, playing a boisterous game of keep-away with a baseball cap. After two of them barreled into a table, a manager came out from behind the counter and ordered them outside.

"High-school kids," Zach sneered as he watched them leave. "There should be a curfew that forbids anyone under eighteen from being out after eight o'clock." Jessica smiled stiffly as Zach readjusted himself in his chair. "I'm just so glad that's all behind me, aren't you? Graduation day was one of the happiest days of my life. I didn't shed a tear at the thought of leaving all those stupid people behind," Zach finished scornfully.

Jessica's stomach lurched. *I'm one of those stupid people,* a voice inside her head screamed. *There's no way I can tell him I'm in high school now.*

Jessica sat up straight in her seat. "So what classes are you taking?" she asked, wanting to steer the conversation to a safer topic.

Zach explained that because he was a premed student, it didn't really matter what his major was, as long as he took plenty of biology. So as a math major, he was taking mostly math, physics, and biology classes to prepare for medical school.

"But for fun I'm taking a really cool philosophy class," Zach said.

"Fun? Philosophy?" Jessica asked dubiously. "You can't be serious."

"I'm totally serious," Zach replied. "The professor is eccentric and brilliant, and there's usually a pretty heated discussion. If you've never taken a philosophy class, you should come sit in on it sometime. In fact, what are you doing tomorrow at noon?"

"Going with you to your favorite philosophy class," Jessica promised.

"And then you can take me to *your* favorite class," Zach suggested.

"I don't think I can use the word 'favorite' to describe any of my classes," Jessica said quickly. "Academics have never really been my thing." Then she realized her mistake—she was supposed to be a former Princeton student. "I mean, I'm good at school, but I don't get too excited about it."

Zach raised an eyebrow. "So what *do* you get excited about?" he asked with a rakish grin.

Jessica narrowed her eyes. "You watch what you're thinking, Zachary Marsden," she said, wagging a finger at him in mock disapproval.

"What's on *your* mind, Jessica Wakefield?" Zach asked, feigning insult. "I was simply asking what you like to do in your spare time."

Jessica smiled. Cheerleading was her favorite pastime, but unfortunately, she couldn't let Zach know she was cocaptain of her high-school cheerleading squad. People had such misconceptions about cheerleaders. Especially blond cheerleaders. *They think we're all dumb, shallow, and preoccupied with boys,* Jessica thought resentfully. *I may be somewhat preoccupied with boys, but I'm certainly not shallow or dumb.*

Jessica wanted Zach to think of her as deep and thoughtful, even intellectual. "Actually, I was into drama all through high school," she said, straightening her spine and crossing her legs to give herself a more regal demeanor.

"Oh, so you're a thespian," Zach said.

"Sure am," Jessica answered proudly. *Thespian,* she

repeated in her mind. She liked the word—it sounded so professional. "I'm just going to college to have something to fall back on—just in case I don't make it as an actress right away. You know, to make myself more marketable," she said, hearing the unmistakable voice of Ned Wakefield. "And to please my dad."

"I hear that," Zach replied with a chuckle. "Sometimes I don't know which one of us decided that I should be a doctor—me or my father. So," he continued, "what plays have you done?"

"My junior year in high school I played Lady Mac—"

Two girls suddenly appeared at their table. "Oh, *there* you are!" a petite girl with a mess of curly black hair said to Zach. "We missed you in study group tonight."

"Right, I'm sorry," Zach stammered. "I had—uh—something came up."

"Looks that way," an athletic-looking blond girl said snippily. "Oh, well, we could have used your help on the *anatomy* homework." They broke into a burst of giggles and walked away.

Zach shook his head. "I hope you don't take this the wrong way, but some girls are so ditzy, it's annoying. That's what I like about you," Zach said. "You're so mature, and you're not afraid to show how smart you are." Zach let his knee touch Jessica's under the table. "Intelligent women are so sexy." He looked at Jessica so appreciatively that she felt as if she would burst with pride.

* * *

Elizabeth, Billie, and Steven were still sitting in the Coffee House when Ian Cooke walked up to their table.

"Hey, Elizabeth—fancy meeting you here!" Ian said.

"Ian, hi!" Elizabeth replied, flashing him a wide smile.

"Listen, that sure was a great party last night. When's the next one?" he asked.

Steven jumped out of his chair. "That's it!" he shouted, looking as if he might turn the table upside down.

Elizabeth stood up quickly. "Ian, let's go over here," she said, leading Ian away from the table. "I'll be back in a minute," she said to Billie, who was pulling Steven back down to sit.

"What'd I say?" Ian asked, confused. Elizabeth explained the situation.

Ian broke into giggles when she described the way Steven and Billie had come home early and discovered that their apartment had turned into a cross between a garbage dump and a septic tank. "I'm sorry, I shouldn't laugh," he said.

"It's OK. I guess it does sound pretty silly."

"But wait," Ian said suddenly. "You're only a senior in high school? I can't believe it."

Elizabeth shrugged her shoulders and smiled. She hadn't told him the *whole* truth, figuring this small lie was OK. She didn't want to seem too much like a baby.

"I have to say, I am disappointed," he continued. "I was looking forward to getting to know you better."

"Why can't you still?" Elizabeth asked.

"I don't know," Ian said. "How would your older brother feel about your dating a college guy? Not to mention your parents."

Elizabeth gulped. Ian *did* like her. She had to tell him she had a boyfriend.

"Actually, Ian," Elizabeth started, "I should let you know that I have a boyfriend—a serious one."

Ian smiled sadly. "I can't say I'm surprised," he said. "In fact, if you were single, I'd have to wonder what was wrong with the male population."

Elizabeth laughed. "I'd still like to come with you to your journalism class, if that's OK," she said.

"Of course it's OK," Ian assured her. "Just because I can't date you doesn't mean I can't encourage your journalism career. In fact, why don't we meet a few minutes before class so I can introduce you to Professor Newkirk? She's a good person for a budding reporter to know."

"I'll be there," Elizabeth promised. Returning to the table, Elizabeth realized how happy she was to have met Ian. He seemed genuine, and genuinely interested in becoming her friend. A lot of times guys backed off when they found out that she had a boyfriend. *Lucky for* me *Ian is different,* Elizabeth thought.

* * *

A lanky guy came up to Zach and Jessica's table. "Zach! Can I borrow your notes from Friday's physics class?"

"Sure, give me a minute to find them," Zach replied.

While Zach fumbled in his bag for his notes, Jessica sat back and let herself relax. She had been a little tense about coming to a college hangout, worried that she might look totally out of place.

But besides the fact that she seemed to be the only girl in the restaurant who was not dressed all in black, she fit right in.

It's all attitude, she realized, crossing one ankle over the other as she saw many of the other girls doing. *No one would ever know that I'm only sixteen years old and a junior in high school.*

Zach looked shyly at Jessica after the guy had walked away. "I guess it wasn't such a great idea to come to one of my regular hangouts," he said. "We're not getting much privacy."

"No, it's OK—I like it here," Jessica said. She wasn't too hip on the whole juice thing, but she did like the fact that everyone seemed to know Zach. "I just hope I have as easy a time meeting people as you seem to. It's always hard to make friends in a new place." Jessica smiled to herself when she played back her last words in her head. *Lila would laugh out loud if she heard me say I'm worried about making friends.* Being popular was the last thing Jessica Wakefield would ever have to worry about.

But she had to play up the transfer-student story.

"I'm sure you'll have no problem making friends," Zach assured her. "Besides, I heard that half of Sweet Valley High's senior class ends up here every year. Don't you know lots of people from high school?"

"Nobody I like," Jessica answered.

The next thing she knew, Henry Jones, a guy who'd been a couple years ahead of her at SVH, walked in. Even though she'd been just a sophomore when he was a senior, Jessica had never been inconspicuous, so there was a pretty good chance Henry would remember her as a junior cheerleader. She ducked her head, hoping Henry would order takeout. Her heart sank when she saw him heading straight for their table.

"Henry! How're you doing, man?" Zach called out.

This calls for drastic action, Jessica thought desperately. Her eye fell on the juice she had barely touched. With a sudden move of her arm she knocked the glass over, spilling the liquid onto her lap.

She jumped out of her seat. "I can't believe it!" she exclaimed. "I better run to the bathroom before the stain sets." Keeping her head down, she pushed past Henry. "Excuse me," she mumbled.

Her relief at escaping soon vanished when she saw the mark that the horrid juice had left on her new sweater. *Now I really wish I had worn black,* she lamented. She scrubbed furiously at the stain. *I just hope Henry's gone by the time I get back.*

No such luck. Henry had taken a seat at their table. *What am I going to do?* Jessica wondered, beginning to panic. *If Zach finds out I'm in high school, he'll never want to speak with me again. He said he hates high-school students. This could ruin everything!* She contemplated ditching Zach and then explaining her disappearance later. But before she could act, Zach caught sight of her over Henry's shoulder. He smiled, looking so happy to see her again that she couldn't even think of leaving.

She positioned herself directly behind Henry—out of his line of vision. "I think I left the stove on," she blurted, cringing at the stupidity of her lie. "I need to get home. Immediately." She started backing out toward the door.

But it was too late. Henry turned around, a flash of recognition appearing in his eyes. "Aren't you—?"

"Jessica Wakefield," she cut him off. "We met on the beach this summer." She held her breath.

"Really? Are you sure? I don't think that's where I know you from," he said. He squinted his eyes at her, still looking as if he were trying to place her.

"Zach! Can we go now?"

"Sure, Jess," Zach said agreeably. "The lady calls—gotta go," he said to Henry as he gathered his things. Walking out the door, Jessica looked over her shoulder to see Henry watching them, a puzzled expression on his face.

"So is Henry a good friend of yours?" she asked innocently when they got outside. She hoped not.

Henry would soon remember where he knew her from, and if he talked to Zach again, he'd probably tell him.

"Not really. I don't hang out that much with freshmen—they're a little annoying," Zach said. Then he gasped. "I mean, not all freshmen."

Jessica smiled weakly. "So where should we go now?" she asked.

Zach raised his eyebrows in surprise. "Don't you want to head back to your apartment? To turn off the stove?"

"Oh, right, that." But Jessica didn't want the date to end just yet. "I just made that up so I wouldn't hurt Henry's feelings," she explained. "No offense, but I really don't like him that much. And besides, I was getting tired of sharing you."

Zach slipped his arm possessively over Jessica's shoulders. "No offense taken," he said cheerfully.

Elizabeth, Steven, and Billie came back to the apartment to find the door unlocked. "I could have sworn I'd locked it," Steven said, confused. "Wait here," he whispered to Elizabeth and Billie. "Let me go in first and make sure there isn't a burglar inside or something."

He reappeared after a minute. "Everything seems to be fine," he said, turning on the overhead light.

"What happened to Jessica?" Billie said when they saw the empty living room. Elizabeth groaned inwardly.

While Billie and Steven checked for her in the bedroom, Elizabeth contemplated what to do. She knew Jessica had been faking the headache to get out of going to the lecture. And she had a feeling her sister had had other plans—namely meeting up with that cute fraternity guy she'd been talking to for hours at the party. Zach, she remembered Jessica had called him.

Elizabeth was in no mood to cover for Jessica again. But if Steven found out the truth, it would be back to high school for both of them. *How could Jessica be so careless?* Elizabeth wondered angrily. Considering how upset Steven had been, Elizabeth had thought Jessica might keep herself under control. *I guess I should know better by now,* she thought ruefully.

"This just keeps getting more and more frustrating!" Steven cried, storming out of the bedroom.

"What do you think happened to her?" Billie asked Elizabeth.

"She probably just got bored and went to a movie or something," Elizabeth said. "I heard her mention how much she wanted to see this new action movie that opened this weekend."

"I thought she had a killer headache," Steven said, looking suspicious.

Whoops! Elizabeth thought.

"Maybe it's really bad and she went to the health clinic," Billie said, looking worried. "We'd better call the infirmary and see if she's there. Liz, would you mind getting me the campus directory in the kitchen?"

"No problem," Elizabeth said. Once in the kitchen, Elizabeth moved fast, scribbling a note in her sister's handwriting. She walked back into the living room.

"Look—I found this note on the counter," she said, handing it to Steven. "I guess I was right. I had a feeling she just didn't want to come to the lecture."

Steven read the note and crumpled it up with a sigh. "Now I know why Mom and Dad sent you guys up here," he said. "They needed a *vacation*."

Elizabeth smiled wanly. *I'm going to kill Jessica,* she thought. *And no jury on earth would ever convict me.*

Jessica hadn't meant to stay out so late, but after the juice bar Zach had suggested a nighttime tour of campus. It wasn't until she heard the clock tower chime ten times that Jessica realized how late it was. And by that time, Steven, Billie, and Elizabeth had surely got home.

So she stalled Zach, knowing that Elizabeth would probably make up some excuse for her. She figured it was better to stay out until Billie and Steven had gone to sleep so that she could get her story straight with Elizabeth.

Now, as she opened the door to Billie and Steven's apartment, Jessica was relieved to find all the lights off. She shut the door softly behind her, listening for sounds of someone stirring. But the coast was clear. Tiptoeing through the silence, Jessica felt too wound up to sleep. But there was nothing else to do but go to bed.

She slipped into the nightshirt that Elizabeth had set out for her on the chair and crawled into the creaky sofa bed, setting the mattress bouncing on its weak springs. Elizabeth stirred and shifted.

"Is that you, Jess?" she mumbled sleepily.

"Of course it's me, you goof!" Jessica answered, happy that Elizabeth had woken. She was bursting to tell her all about her wonderful date. "Liz, I had the most fantastic time tonight!"

Elizabeth groaned.

Lying on her back, Jessica clasped her hands together behind her head and stared up at the ceiling. "Zach is the most interesting, mature, thoughtful boy I've ever dated in my life. I can't wait for you to meet him. I think even you're going to like him," she whispered. "I bet he's even smarter than your nerdy friend, Ian."

"Jess, would you do me a favor and shut up?" Elizabeth grumbled. She rolled onto her stomach and raised herself on her elbows, glaring down at Jessica's placid face. "First of all, I'm really tired after the long day we had cleaning up the mess you caused with your stupid party. Second of all, I'm furious that you forced me to cover for you again tonight," she whispered harshly. "So the last thing I want to do right now is hear about your two-timing Ken!" With that Elizabeth rolled over, leaving Jessica with a view of her back.

Jessica raised her eyebrows. *Two-timing Ken? Is that what I'm doing?* She started to feel the beginning of her least-favorite emotion: guilt. Then she heard the bedroom door open and close, and Billie appeared, dressed in her robe.

"I thought I heard some talking out here," Billie said, pulling an ottoman up to the side of the sofa bed.

"I'm sorry, Billie," Elizabeth apologized, sitting up. "Did we wake you?"

"It's OK, really. I couldn't sleep," she said. She looked at Jessica. "I was worried about you."

"Well, I'm fine," Jessica replied. She was not up for a lecture from Billie, too.

"I can see that," Billie said. Even in the dark Jessica could see the serious expression on her face. "I know you're up to something. I don't know what it is, but I knew you had something planned when you used the old headache excuse."

Jessica gulped. *Is Billie going to spill everything to Steven?*

"I also know what you're worried about," she continued, "and the answer is no, I'm not going to say anything to Steven."

Jessica breathed a sigh of relief. "Thanks, Billie."

"I know that Steven's like an overprotective father with you two," Billie said. "He doesn't seem to understand how important it is to let the people he loves make their own mistakes."

Jessica felt elated. She had no idea that Billie would be such an ally. "It's so wonderful that you understand, Billie," Jessica said out loud. "With all of the stuff we've done, I'll bet Liz and I are more mature than most of the college kids here. People shouldn't treat us like children."

Billie continued as if Jessica hadn't said anything. "You girls are adults and have a right to lead your own lives." She gave Jessica a meaningful look. "As long as you don't do anything really stupid."

Jessica returned her look, unflinching. *There's nothing stupid about making a wonderful man fall in love with me. What could possibly go wrong?* she thought confidently. *I've got everything under control.*

Chapter 9

"It was really nice of the Thetas to invite me, but I don't think I'll be able to make it to tea this afternoon," Elizabeth said to Jessica as they walked across the quad the next morning.

"I can't believe you're not absolutely jumping at the chance to have tea at Theta," Jessica said. "I thought you'd be as thrilled as I am."

"There are just so many other things I want to do during my short time here at SVU," Elizabeth explained.

"Like what?" Jessica demanded. "What's so important that you can't spend one measly hour having tea and crumpets?"

Elizabeth looked at her sister and rolled her eyes. "I can think of a *lot* of more important things to do than having tea and crumpets with a bunch of sorority snobs," she said with a grin.

"They're not snobs, Liz," Jessica said, sounding hurt. "I can't believe you'd even say that when you don't even know them."

"You're right," Elizabeth said. "I don't know them. I'm sorry—I'm sure they're very nice."

"They are," Jessica defended her new friends.

"But we're not even going to be here for another two years," Elizabeth argued. "I don't want to waste an afternoon on something that won't even matter until we're freshmen. Besides, I'm not even sure I want to rush once I do come here."

Jessica gasped. "Are you serious, Liz?" she exclaimed. "But you have to rush. We're a team." Jessica took Elizabeth by the hand. "Being a Theta wouldn't mean anything to me if you weren't there with me," she said earnestly.

Elizabeth smiled. "Stop pouting," she said. "It causes frown lines, remember?" Elizabeth nudged Jessica playfully—that was something Lila always said.

When Jessica smiled at her joke, Elizabeth said, "That's better. All right, if it's that important to you, I'll go with you to Theta House for tea."

"Thanks, Liz!" Jessica said enthusiastically. "And we'll have so much fun—I promise!"

As soon as they reached the student union, the twins split up. Elizabeth went downstairs to find the office for the school paper, while Jessica went in search of information about football games and cheerleading tryouts.

On her way to the student-athletics office, Jessica spotted a performing-arts bulletin board. She decided to look for notices announcing auditions for school plays, and bands looking for lead singers.

Jessica stopped short when she saw a girl standing in front of the board, scribbling in her notebook. With her long, wavy honey-colored hair, the girl reminded Jessica of Heather Mallone, cocaptain of the cheerleading team and Jessica's number-one enemy at Sweet Valley High. *And the competition,* Jessica added to herself. *I wonder if Zach finds girls like that attractive.*

Suddenly she felt the hairs on the back of her neck stand up. She had the eerie sensation that she was being watched.

"Thinking of making your grand debut in this winter's production?" a sexy voice behind her said.

Jessica wheeled around to come face-to-face with Zach. "Zach! I was just thinking about you!" she said, her face breaking into a huge grin.

Zach laughed out loud. "You were not. You were plotting the quickest way to grab center stage at SVU—by eliminating the competition," he said with a lopsided grin.

Jessica smiled. "Actually, I was doing both—thinking about you and checking out the competition." Then she amended hastily, "But that's not usual for me, honestly." She didn't want him to think she was too catty.

"Don't worry, Jess," Zach said, giving her cheek a

light stroke. "I like a girl who won't let anyone get in the way of her goals."

Jessica was elated. Instead of being turned off by her competitive streak, Zach seemed to like it. *I bet he's exactly the same way,* she thought.

Zach glanced at his watch. "I have to run, but can I carry your books to your next class?"

Uh-oh, Jessica thought. Noticing the huge backpack on Zach's shoulder, Jessica realized how weird it must look that she had no books. And no class to go to. "Monday's my light load—I just have one afternoon seminar," she explained quickly. "I was just stopping here on my way to do some errands."

Zach seemed satisfied with the explanation. "I hope you're still planning to come with me to that philosophy class."

"Of course! I've been looking forward to it!" Jessica replied enthusiastically, just as Elizabeth walked up to them. Elizabeth snorted and Jessica kicked her in the shin.

"Zach, this is my sister, Elizabeth," Jessica said. "I'm just showing her around campus today."

"Nice to meet you," Zach greeted Elizabeth. "Jessica's been telling me about you. How do you like our fair campus so far?"

"It's nice," Elizabeth said, looking puzzled.

Jessica had to get rid of Zach before he started asking too many questions. "Well, I don't want to be the one to make you late for class," she said, giving Zach a kiss on the cheek. "I'll see you later."

Zach had barely left the building before Elizabeth turned on Jessica. "What was that about *you* showing *me* around campus?" she demanded.

Jessica paused. She figured she'd better come clean. "I was just about to explain that to you," she said.

"Start explaining, Jessica Wakefield," Elizabeth said, folding her arms across her chest.

"I kind of told Zach that I'm in college and you're my younger sister," Jessica blurted, bracing herself for her sister's wrath.

"You did *what?*" Elizabeth shouted. A few students turned to look at the twins.

"Ssh, people are looking at us," Jessica whispered.

"I don't care who's looking at us," Elizabeth said sternly. "Of all the ridiculous things you've done in your life, this has got to be the worst."

"Oh, Liz. Don't get so excited—it's harmless," Jessica said. "So how was the school paper?" She didn't give a hoot about the school paper, but she wanted to distract Elizabeth from the disapproving speech that she was sure was on the tip of her twin's tongue.

Jessica's diversionary tactic worked. Elizabeth must have been bursting to tell Jessica all about how one of the producers from the campus television station was recruiting in the newspaper office, because she blurted it all out in a flood. Jessica paid half-hearted attention as Elizabeth explained that in the past the television station had been a bare-bones venture, but some alumnus who had made it big in broadcasting had donated money to fund a much more ambitious program.

Elizabeth's eyes were shining. "The thought of venturing into broadcast journalism is really exciting, especially since I've been reading all about Edward R. Murrow."

Jessica raised an eyebrow. "Liz, I'm surprised at you. I thought the glamorous world of TV news would be beneath your dignity," she teased.

That spurred Elizabeth to launch into a lengthy explanation about how she'd like to get involved in making television news more responsible. Jessica stifled a yawn and looked at her watch. "Liz! Hate to cut you off, but didn't you say you were meeting Ian at ten forty-five?"

Elizabeth gasped. "See you!" she said, running off.

She's awfully excited to meet up with Ian, Jessica thought as she watched her sister break into a full run. *I wonder what Todd would say if he knew his girlfriend was making dates with college guys.*

Suddenly a picture of Ken's smiling face popped into her mind. *That's different,* she told herself, pushing the vision from her thoughts. *That's totally different.*

I can't believe I let myself lose track of the minutes, Elizabeth chastised herself. The huge face of the clock on Kerr Hall taunted her with the time. *Eleven-oh-five. I promised Ian I'd meet him at ten forty-five. He must think I'm such a flake.*

Panting and out of breath, Elizabeth finally made it to the Dwight School of Journalism, a brown-shingled building with white trim and green ivy spread upon its surface. It was actually off campus—across the street from the very westernmost point, on a grassy knoll lined by trees.

Elizabeth fell in love with the place the minute she laid eyes on it. It was a rambling, ramshackle mansion with a wraparound porch. A handful of students sat talking on the wide front steps, and two couples rocked gently in the porch swings. *I could see myself spending a lot of time here,* Elizabeth mused.

Elizabeth's reverie ended abruptly when she realized that Ian was nowhere to be found among the students. She dreaded the thought of walking into Felicia Newkirk's class late.

Ever since she'd found out that the famed journalist was a professor there, Elizabeth had been fantasizing about their first meeting. She was hoping to make a really good impression, imagining that Felicia would turn out to be the mentor she'd always wanted.

But how was it going to look if she walked into her class late and out of breath? *It will look like I'm an irresponsible child, that's how it will look,* Elizabeth thought.

"And what have we here?" Felicia Newkirk leaned forward on the podium, glaring over the rims of her glasses. Elizabeth recognized the portly woman from her appearances on public-television talk shows. *She looks much more intimidating in real life,* Elizabeth realized.

She felt her face turn a bright shade of red as everyone turned around to look at her. "I'm sorry I'm late, Ms. Newkirk," Elizabeth apologized, letting the door slip shut behind her. Spotting Ian in the back row, Elizabeth smiled weakly and made her way to the seat he had held open for her.

"Not only are you tardy, young lady, but I believe you are in the wrong classroom," Ms. Newkirk said haughtily, straightening the big bow of her bright-red blouse. "This is an advanced journalism class."

"Um, I, he, we—" Elizabeth stammered.

Ian stood up. "This is Elizabeth Wakefield, Professor Newkirk. I invited her to sit in on your class because she's a huge fan of yours, and a journalist in her own right."

"Oh, are you, now?" said Professor Newkirk, eyeing Elizabeth with scorn. "Did you hear that, class? We have the great fortune of having a budding young journalist in our midst."

Elizabeth burned at Professor Newkirk's patronizing tone, trying not to let herself get flustered. Then she sat up straight in her chair. "Actually, I've had quite a bit of experience." She listed off an abbreviated description of her credits, highlighting her internship with the London *Times* and her ambitions to become a professional journalist. "In fact, I was delayed coming to class today because I was talking to a producer with the school's TV station."

Professor Newkirk snorted. "Isn't that fitting? Our young journalist wants to be on TV," she said sarcastically.

"It's not that I just want to be on TV, Ms. New—er, Professor Newkirk," Elizabeth said, biting her tongue for not using the more respectful title. "I've been strictly a print journalist so far, and I'd just like to try broadcast journalism for a change."

Professor Newkirk smiled sardonically. "Oh, I see. So you find print journalism boring."

"I didn't say that!" Elizabeth cried. "I just—what's so—" she sputtered. Her fatigue from having lost sleep seemed to be overwhelming her ability to speak. She cursed Jessica for having kept her awake the night before, going on and on about Zach.

Professor Newkirk jumped on Elizabeth's show of weakness. "I've seen more good journalists make utter fools of themselves by agreeing to banter on silly talk shows that masquerade as intelligent discussions. That's why I refuse to even appear on commercial television," she said, fussing with what Elizabeth was sure was a bad wig. "Broadcast journalism is merely trumped-up entertainment packaged to sell advertising," she said expansively. A number of students nodded their agreement.

Elizabeth rose to the argument. "I think—I mean a lot of people think—a lot of respected journalists think—" Why couldn't she find the words to form her argument? "When used responsibly, TV journalism can be really good," she finally blurted.

"I see. And I suppose you think you're just the kind of responsible journalist who could make it *good,*" Professor Newkirk said in a mocking tone.

Against her better judgment, Elizabeth stood up to defend herself. "You have no right to patronize me like that," she said, ignoring Ian's warning glare. "I'm just as good a journalist as any of your so-called advanced students."

"Well, I don't know about that, but at least you're pretty—that's all a girl like you will need, anyway, especially on TV. As long as you have a script in front of you, I'm sure you'll do fine." Professor Newkirk turned back to the papers on her podium, as if she considered the topic closed.

Now Elizabeth was angry. She hated it when people thought that just because she was pretty, she didn't have a brain in her head. But from the way she was behaving today, she had to admit she'd probably write herself off as a dumb blonde, too.

Elizabeth knew she should just shut up, but she couldn't restrain herself. "Print journalists are no better or more noble than the TV reporters they despise," she said. "I think most of them are just jealous of the money and the glory."

Professor Newkirk turned around and raised her eyebrows, but said nothing. Elizabeth sat back down, willing her blood to stop pumping vigorously through her veins. The other students shifted uncomfortably in their seats, and Elizabeth felt the heat Ian was giving off as he glowered next to her.

"Well," Professor Newkirk finally huffed with an exaggerated release of air. "Let's move on." She announced that she was giving the class a special assignment: a one-thousand-word piece on college life. "Actually, it's not just an assignment, it's a competition, and not a voluntary one. All papers must be on my desk by nine tomorrow morning." Everyone let out a groan.

"Oh, stop your whining," Professor Newkirk scolded. "If you want to be journalists, you're going to have to get used to tight deadlines." Then she told them that the winner—and the prize—would be announced at the Tuesday-night seminar, followed by the guest speaker they usually had at that time.

Professor Newkirk gazed at Elizabeth over her horn-rimmed glasses. "I presume you'll be participating, Ms. Wakefield?"

Elizabeth's heart dropped. What did she know about college life? Then she noticed that all the students in the class were staring at her. If she backed down, she'd look like a fool—to Professor Newkirk, to Ian, and to the rest of the advanced journalism students. She knew she was as good as they were.

"Of course," she said out loud. "I'd be honored to participate." *And my essay's going to show you just how wrong you are about me,* she vowed silently.

After picking up a notebook at the student bookstore to give her more of a college image, Jessica met

Zach in front of the school of philosophy. Walking into class with him, Jessica noticed Billie's unmistakable chestnut hair down in the front row.

"Let's sit back here," she whispered quickly, nudging Zach toward two empty chairs in the back.

Zach shook his head. "Actually, Jess, I usually like to sit up front," he said. "When I sit in back, I have trouble following. C'mon." Jessica stood paralyzed as Zach bounded down the risers, settling into a chair two seats away from Billie. *What am I going to do? Of all the philosophy classes he could take, Zach had to go and choose Billie's,* Jessica lamented.

When Zach realized that Jessica hadn't followed him, he turned around and motioned for her to join him. *It's no use,* she thought. *It would look really weird if I took a seat in the back all by myself.*

Moving slowly toward Zach, Jessica realized that there was a way to work this situation to her advantage. After all, she was supposed to be enrolled in school there. She should know at least someone on campus. She decided to take control of the potentially disastrous coincidence.

"Billie! I didn't know you were taking this class!" Jessica exclaimed. Billie looked up and opened her mouth in surprise.

Jessica continued speaking before Billie had a chance to say anything. "If I'd known, I would have followed you in here ages ago. I've heard this professor's lectures are fantastic."

"Jess, what—" Billie started.

"Zach, I'd like you to meet Billie, a friend of mine from back east," Jessica said, stressing the last two words in the hopes that Billie would clue in to the fact that she was lying. Before their conversation the previous night, Jessica would never have thought she could count on Billie's support.

"Hi, I'm Billie," she said haltingly, holding out her hand to Zach.

"Good to meet you," Zach said, shaking her hand. "Are you a transfer student, too?"

Billie looked startled. "No," she said, her eyebrows scrunched together in puzzlement.

"Zach's a transfer student like me," Jessica jumped in. "We met on Saturday—at the party," Jessica said, holding Billie's gaze.

"Oh," Billie said. She still looked puzzled, but fortunately, at that moment the professor entered the classroom. Everyone faced forward when he cleared his throat to start the lecture.

Jessica was surprised to find that she was actually interested in the lecture. It was all about truth and desire. She especially liked it when the professor argued that it was a self-evident truth that a person ought to desire whatever is truly good for him-or herself. *Little did I know that my way of thinking has been around since Plato,* she thought with a grin.

After the lecture Billie turned to Jessica. "Do you guys want to come back to the apartment with me for lunch?"

"Thanks, Billie, but I have to go to the registration

office before my tea at Theta House. The registrar keeps giving me grief about transferring here halfway through the semester," Jessica said. *Come on, Billie, figure it out,* she added silently.

Finally Billie's face broke into a knowing smile. "OK. Maybe we can get together later this week, after you've got all your classes sorted out." Billie packed up her bag, shaking her head. As she stood up to leave, she gave Jessica a bemused smile.

Jessica smiled right back, congratulating herself on her quick thinking. *If I can dig myself out of that one, it's going to be smooth sailing from here on out,* she thought with relief.

Chapter 10

"I can't spend the afternoon with you, Zach. I have a date for tea at Theta House," Jessica said, trying to extract her hand from Zach's grip. They were sitting on a bench in the quad, having just finished eating the sandwiches they'd picked up for lunch.

Jessica had been trying to leave him for the last twenty minutes, and she still had to go back to the apartment to change. Looking into his beautiful green eyes, she felt sick at the thought of leaving him. But her tea date was important. Theta was her future. "Please believe me when I say that if it were anything but Theta House, I would blow it off in a minute to spend more time with you."

"OK, I'll let you go," Zach finally relented, still holding on to her hand. "But only if you promise to have dinner with me tonight."

Jessica willingly agreed.

* * *

Jessica rushed back to Steven's apartment and changed quickly into the outfit she had picked out. Now she sat in the kitchen, feeling her tension rise every time the hands on the kitchen clock lurched forward. Elizabeth had promised to meet her at the apartment at two o'clock so they could walk over to the sorority house together, but so far there was no sign of her twin.

"Where is that flaky sister of mine?" she whispered under her breath, laughing to herself at how silly it sounded to describe Elizabeth as flaky. In most cases it was Jessica who didn't give a second's thought to being late. But this was different. Sorority girls were notorious for knocking you down for every little thing.

Finally she realized she'd better give up on Elizabeth and head for the Theta House by herself. *Elizabeth is certainly going to hear about this,* Jessica swore.

Jessica stopped fretting about Elizabeth the minute she rounded the corner and found herself on Cherry Lane, the street that was otherwise known as Greek Row. It was a wide, winding avenue, divided down the center by long patches of grass that were speckled with tiny bright flowers.

Every house was a mansion, each one more impressive than the last. Jessica gasped out loud when she realized which one was number 3461, the address of Theta Alpha Theta. It was a crisp redbrick three-story building with four majestic white columns that stretched the length of the entire facade. The front garden was impeccably groomed, from the lush green lawn to the clipped hedges that edged the building. *It's the most beautiful mansion on the street,* she thought in awe.

I could see myself spending a lot of time here, Jessica mused as she knocked.

Jessica was happy to see a familiar face open the door. "It's absolutely fabulous to see you again," Darcy Frey gushed. She was one of the girls who had been at Jessica's party.

"It's great to be here," Jessica said sincerely, taking in Darcy's casual but stylish outfit: khakis and a sleeveless green cotton sweater that looked great with her wavy auburn hair. *Much different from the hot little number she wore to my party,* Jessica thought, remembering that this was the girl who had danced with her on top of the coffee table.

"Come on in," Darcy said, opening the big door wide. "We're all hanging out in the parlor."

Jessica walked under a huge crystal chandelier and past a grand stairway to the open archway of the front parlor. About a dozen girls were chatting in small groups throughout the large room, sitting on chairs and sofas, a few sitting on the floor.

Jessica appreciated the room's tasteful decor—the walls were all painted a pale shade of peach, and the furniture and carpet were color coordinated to match.

"Girls, I'd like you all to meet Jessica Wakefield," Darcy announced in a loud voice, silencing the many conversations going on at once.

"So *this* is Jessica Wakefield," a girl said in a contemptuous tone. Jessica didn't recognize her. "We've been hearing a lot about you." The girl let her gray eyes wander up and down, taking in Jessica's outfit. A few of the girls giggled. Feeling conspicuously overdressed in her teal linen suit, Jessica felt her upper lip break out into a sweat. *What have they heard?* she wondered, suddenly worried. She realized with a start that she was actually nervous about meeting these girls. She couldn't remember ever feeling so much pressure to make a good impression.

Relax, she commanded herself. *The fastest way to make a bad impression is to seem insecure.* "Nothing bad, I imagine," she said lightly, smiling wide to show off her dimple.

"And why would you think otherwise? Is there anything we should know?" the girl with gray eyes asked, raising an eyebrow in a perfect arch.

"Stop it, Meredith," Darcy said. She touched Jessica on the arm. "Meredith takes it upon herself to make every new rush feel inferior, doesn't she?" A few of the girls nodded and groaned.

"I'm just teasing," Meredith said. "You can take it, can't you, Jessica?"

"Of course I can take it," Jessica answered. *And I can dish it out, too,* she added silently.

"We just heard all about your raging party on Saturday night," one girl explained.

"And that you're Alice Wakefield's daughter," another said. That started conversation buzzing about the twins' mother.

"Is she still as gorgeous as she was when she was a student here?" Darcy asked after Jessica had pointed out her mother's face in an old black-and-white picture hanging on the wall.

"Actually, she looks a lot like me," Jessica replied. "In fact, people often mistake her for Liz's and my sister."

"Where *is* Elizabeth?" Meredith asked. "I thought for sure she'd want to introduce herself to Theta House, too."

Stunned, Jessica's mind went blank. Why hadn't she thought up an excuse on her way there? Of course they would think it odd that Elizabeth hadn't shown. Every girl should jump at the chance to meet the Thetas. They absolutely could not know the truth: that Elizabeth had flaked.

But Jessica was always quick on her feet. "Elizabeth was totally excited about coming, but she found out that today's the only day to audition to be an on-air personality for the student TV station. Have you heard about it? It's really exciting." Jessica prattled on, making Elizabeth out to be a regular Ricki Lake. The girls were impressed, and no one questioned how Elizabeth could work for the college TV station when she was still in high school. *Liz had better thank me,* Jessica said to herself.

Steven felt as if he were back in high school, skipping class to go kiss a girl out behind the gym.

"I feel like we're doing something totally naughty. For some reason I'm scared of getting punished if we get caught," Billie said, giggling mischievously.

"I was just thinking the same thing," Steven said, happy that Billie shared his feelings about this adventure. To make up for their disaster of a weekend, Steven and Billie had decided to do the unthinkable—forgo their afternoon classes to spend a romantic afternoon in their apartment. They had stopped at their favorite deli, hoping to re-create the magic they had felt on the beach Saturday night, before the rain clouds had spoiled the mood.

Billie went to the kitchen to get a bottle of sparkling cider out of the refrigerator while Steven pulled the curtains, put on his CD recording of waves crashing against the shore, and placed candles around the room.

"The twins won't be back for hours," Steven said as he spread a picnic blanket on the floor. "They're having tea at Theta House, and you know how girls can gossip for hours on end."

Billie looked at Steven crossly. "Steven—"

"Just kidding," Steven said before she could scold him.

Billie laughed. "Come here, you," she said,

pulling him into an embrace. Things were hot and heavy between them in a matter of minutes.

All of a sudden the lights came on. Elizabeth walked in, oblivious to the scene in the living room. "I don't know how you can say that," she said over her shoulder to someone behind her.

Then Ian walked into the apartment. "I'm sorry, but I happen to agree with Professor Newkirk."

"But if good journalists don't change with the times—" Elizabeth stopped midsentence when she spotted Steven and Billie in a tangle on the floor.

Ian blushed and backed away toward the door. "This apartment is really a happening place," he stammered. "I'll catch you later, Liz." He made a fast getaway.

"Uh, I'll just go use the computer in the bedroom," Elizabeth said after Ian had left. She tried to muffle her giggles with the back of her hand, but she didn't completely succeed.

"Why me?" Steven groaned, rolling onto his back. Billie broke into laughter.

"But I've heard that English literature is a terrible major for meeting guys," Jessica said to Amanda Gregory, the cute blonde who had been at her party.

"There is that," Amanda conceded with a giggle. "But I still think it's the most interesting. I can always change my mind—I'm just a freshman."

"That's true," Jessica said. She was enjoying

herself. Talking to Amanda was helping her feel much more at ease.

Then Magda Helperin walked into the parlor. Jessica hadn't learned until the end of her party that Magda was Theta treasurer. She knew it would be a good move to make friends with one of the officers, so she excused herself from Amanda and walked over to where Magda was sitting alone on a couch.

"Anyone sitting here?" Jessica asked.

Magda looked up and smiled. "Sit right down," she said, patting the couch cushion. "So, Jessica, what do you think of sorority life so far?"

"Actually, I'm already a sorority girl," Jessica answered. "It's not exactly the same, but I'm one of the officers of Phi Beta, the most exclusive sorority at Sweet Valley High."

"High-school sororities are such fun," said Magda, pursing her lips in a prim pout. With her knees locked together and her starched, buttoned-up shirt, Jessica couldn't believe that this was the same girl who had been throwing back beer after beer at her party.

"What else do you do with your time?" Magda asked, taking a sip of her tea.

Jessica was starting to feel as if she were on a job interview, but she didn't let herself get rattled. She proudly informed Magda of her leadership on the cheerleading team, figuring Magda didn't need to know she shared the top spot with Heather Mallone.

"You must have men falling all over you as head

cheerleader," Magda said. Jessica smiled. She had a feeling the conversation would quickly turn to guys.

Magda was duly impressed when Jessica informed her that her boyfriend was the star quarterback and captain of the football team. Then she contemplated telling Magda about Zach. *Would she think I was two-timing my boyfriend?* Jessica wondered, hearing Elizabeth's voice in her head. *Or would she be impressed by the fact that a college man is interested in me?*

She decided to risk it. "There's also this really cute guy I met at my party on Saturday night," she said, winking conspiratorially. "I've been hanging out with him for the last few days."

"A *college* man? Very impressive," Magda said with a toss of her glossy black hair. "One can never have too many men," she proclaimed. Jessica knew she had made the right decision in telling Magda.

"It's nothing serious," Jessica explained. "I mean, I'm really in love with Ken. But it's fun for now."

"And does this college man know you have a boyfriend back in high school?" Magda asked, her crystal-blue eyes sparkling with curiosity.

"Well, no," Jessica admitted. "He's under the impression I'm a student here."

Magda laughed. "I think we'll get along just fine," she said, touching Jessica's knee.

Jessica beamed. "Do you have a boyfriend?" she asked.

"No, not at the moment," Magda said. "But there is someone I've set my sights on."

"Oh, tell me about him," Jessica prompted her.

"Well, he's a transfer student, he's incredibly sexy and smart, and he's premed," Magda said.

Jessica felt her heart leap into her throat. *No, it can't be,* she thought, holding her breath. "What's his name?"

"Zach Marsden. Isn't that a sexy name?" Magda asked, her eyes wide with excitement.

Jessica's smile remained plastered on her face. *Uh-oh,* she thought. *I'm in big trouble.*

Later that night Elizabeth sat at Steven's computer, her face in her hands. She'd been staring at the screen for hours, suffering from a dire case of writer's block. She hadn't even come up with a topic.

It's only one thousand words, Elizabeth kept telling herself. *One word leads to the next one, which leads to the next one.* But it was that first one that seemed to cause her so much trouble.

Elizabeth was terrified of falling flat on her face, especially after that flogging she had received from Professor Newkirk. She had to write the best piece of journalism she'd ever written in her life. But every time she started in on a topic, it came out sounding trite. She racked her brain, trying to think of something fresh. Hearing Jessica humming happily in the bathroom, preparing for her dinner date, Elizabeth considered writing about the attraction college men held for high-school girls. *No,* Elizabeth thought dismissively. *On top of the fact that Jessica would probably kill me, Professor Newkirk would think that topic's silly. And it is.*

Then she thought of the description Jessica had given her of the afternoon at Theta House that Elizabeth had happily missed. Should she write about the pressure girls put on each other in sororities? *Oh, that would go over well with Felicia Newkirk,* she decided sarcastically. *She's already pegged me as a sorority bimbo.*

Speaking of competition, Elizabeth wondered, how about the competitive nature of college athletics? *It's been done, about a thousand times,* she realized dejectedly. The struggles of deciding on a major? *How totally boring,* Elizabeth thought. *I want to impress Professor Newkirk, not put her to sleep.*

Suddenly Elizabeth was overcome with worry. Her head was spinning so fast, there was no way she could possibly be focused that night. And if she didn't write an absolutely spectacular essay, how was she going to make Felicia Newkirk see that she wasn't just another pretty face? Now she knew how Jessica had felt when everyone had thought she'd cheated on the SATs.

Then Elizabeth started feeling the same rush of doubt she had suffered when she'd got her first SAT scores. Before that Elizabeth had never doubted her intelligence. And even though her scores had improved tremendously on the second try, she couldn't quite banish the nagging memory of feeling like a failure. *What if my* first *scores were the real measure of my intelligence? And my* second *scores were the fluke? Maybe I've been fooling myself—and everyone else—all these years. Maybe I just have an average, uncreative brain.* Now close to hysteria, Elizabeth felt a tear drip slowly down her cheek.

To make matters worse, Jessica had been fussing in the bathroom for over an hour. Just when Elizabeth would get used to silence, the blow dryer would start up again.

"Could you keep it down in there?" Elizabeth called out finally. "Your hair must be drier than a desert by now."

Jessica switched the dryer to the low setting. "Excuse me for breathing!" she replied hotly. "My hair is totally misbehaving, so I keep having to wet it and start over again." The dryer switched back to full power.

"Anybody home?" Steven called out suddenly from the living room. Elizabeth hadn't heard him come in over the sound of the dryer.

"I'm in here," Elizabeth answered.

Jessica ran out of the bathroom with a distressed look on her face. "Billie, Steven, what are you doing here?"

"We live here, remember?" Steven reminded her.

"But I thought you'd be out all evening," Jessica said.

"So did I," Elizabeth called from the bedroom. "I

haven't even come close to finishing my essay."

"Well, we're sorry to disturb you girls, but I had to come back because I forgot my logic textbook," Steven said sarcastically.

"So you're leaving?" Jessica asked.

Steven looked at her angrily. "Yes, we're leaving," he said gruffly. That seemed to satisfy Jessica. She went back into the bathroom.

Billie shut the bathroom door to block out the scream of the blow dryer. "How are you doing?" she asked Elizabeth, peeking into the bedroom.

"Terrible," Elizabeth wailed. Billie sat down on the corner of the bed as Elizabeth described her frustration.

"How can I write about college life when I've only been on campus one day?" Elizabeth lamented.

Billie thought for a minute. "You're the writer. But I've always been told that you should write about what you know," she suggested. "Think about something you've experienced personally. Weekends count, too," she said with a wink.

It wasn't until Billie and Steven had left that Elizabeth figured out Billie's hint. While cleaning the apartment on Sunday, Elizabeth and Billie had got into a conversation about how prevalent binge drinking was on campus.

Why didn't I think of that before? Elizabeth admonished herself. *I have firsthand knowledge of one of the most important issues facing college students today: alcohol.*

* * *

"Do you mind if I close the door?" Jessica stood in the doorway of the bedroom, watching Elizabeth's fingers fly over the keyboard.

"Sure," Elizabeth answered brusquely without turning from the computer screen. "Why?"

"Well, Zach's picking me up, and it would look really weird if he saw my younger sister here working," Jessica said quickly.

Elizabeth stopped typing and turned, throwing Jessica a nasty look. But Jessica closed the door before Elizabeth could say anything. A minute later Jessica smiled, hearing the unmistakable click of her twin typing away at the keyboard.

That instant there was a knock on the door. Jessica gasped. *That was a close one!* she thought.

"Wow!" Zach said, looking her up and down after she had opened the door. Jessica was wearing a cropped white sweater over a very short red-and-black-plaid miniskirt, finishing the look with black thigh-highs. From the way he was drinking her in with his eyes, Jessica knew he appreciated all the effort she'd made to look good.

"Where are we going?" Jessica asked after she'd hustled him out of the apartment.

"I thought tonight we could go to Harold's," Zach said. "I figured since you plan on rushing, you'd want to be seen there—it's the favorite Greek hangout."

"Great idea," Jessica agreed readily.

"I brought my car," Zach said, pointing to a cute

red convertible Cabriolet parked on the street.

"No wonder you were asking about driving with the top down!" Jessica said with a laugh.

"I guess I'm pretty transparent," Zach said, smiling shyly.

Jessica kissed him on the cheek. "No, just adorable." Watching Zach walk around the front of the car after he had closed her door, Jessica admired just how adorable he was, dressed in a soft denim shirt and khaki slacks. *We make a great couple,* she thought.

Jessica's mood rose even higher when they pulled up to Harold's Bar and Grill.

"You would never know it was a Monday night from the looks of this place," Jessica said, taking in the high level of activity. The front door didn't stop opening and closing—every time someone left, someone else walked in. *College life seems like one big party,* she thought happily. *I love it.*

"Yeah," Zach said. "Harold's is usually hopping."

They walked up the stairs to the front entrance, with Zach's arm draped casually around her shoulders. He held open the door and Jessica pranced inside, feeling like a real sorority girl.

Then she stopped. Magda was sitting with a bunch of students at a table not twenty feet from the front door. *What was I thinking, coming to a Greek hangout?* Jessica scolded herself. *I can't let Magda see me with Zach!*

"You know, come to think of it, I've changed my

mind," Jessica blurted, backing up into Zach, who was still holding the door behind her. She stepped around him, shielding herself from Magda's view with the door frame. "Let's go somewhere different, away from all the other students." She pulled on Zach's arm until he let the door swing shut behind him. "I don't want to share you with anyone tonight," she cooed, gazing up into his eyes.

"Sure, Jess," Zach said. "I can't argue with that."

Jessica looked back over her shoulder as they walked down the steps. Magda was looking out the window. *Did she see me?* Jessica wondered with dread.

Chapter 11

Steven plunged his spoon into the cup in front of him. "Did you see the smirk on Elizabeth's face when she walked in on us this afternoon?" he asked Billie. "Like we were doing something totally indecent or something," he griped. "You'd think we were stark naked in the middle of the quad at noontime instead of trying to have a private moment in our own home." Steven stirred furiously, watching the white foam of the cappuccino turn slowly beige.

"Steven, that's my cappuccino," Billie said gently, nudging Steven's tea toward him. After they'd had enough of the library, Steven and Billie had gone to the Coffee House to continue their studies. But Steven was having a hard time getting his sisters out of his mind.

"Oh, sorry," Steven said absentmindedly. "And what about the way Jessica lit into us about coming home early tonight! Like it was her right to take over our apartment," he fumed.

"I know, I know," Billie said soothingly. "Please don't bite my head off for saying this, but you're just making yourself even more stressed by dwelling on it. Let's at least try to get some studying done."

"You're right," Steven said, turning his attention back to the legal textbook that sat open in front of him. The book might as well have been written in Latin from the way Steven was struggling to understand it.

"Would you mind stopping that?" Billie said, closing her fingers over Steven's right hand. Steven looked up, puzzled. "You were tapping the table with your pen," she explained.

"Sorry," Steven mumbled, turning back to the book. Suddenly his pen went flying out of his fingers—he had been fiddling with it again. Cursing, he bent to retrieve it. One minute later he accidentally dropped it again.

"It's no use," Steven cried in frustration. "Look at me! I'm a wreck. I don't think I'll be able to focus on school until my two bratty sisters are out of my hair."

Billie looked at Steven. "I'm having trouble concentrating, too," she admitted. "But I don't know if it's because of them or because of you."

Steven looked across the table at his girlfriend, and a feeling of shame washed over him. Not only did Billie have to put up with the twins, she had to deal with him. "I'm so sorry for putting you through this, Billie," Steven said, weaving her fingers between his. "Especially after Oli—"

Billie raised her free hand up to Steven's mouth, stopping him before he could finish. "Sshh," she said. "You promised not to say his name, remember?"

"Right, I'm sorry. I'll stop bringing him up," Steven promised. Then he sat up straight and snapped his fingers. "But now that the topic has already been raised, I just thought of something."

"What's that?" Billie asked.

"What was the absolute worst thing about Oliver's visit?"

Billie heaved her shoulders and sighed a big sigh. "Steven, I thought we agreed not to talk about this."

"No, wait. Just bear with me for a minute. What was the worst thing about his visit?"

Billie rubbed her chin. "The cigarettes?" Steven shook his head. "The late nights?" Steven shook his head again. "I've got it," Billie said. "The fact that he wouldn't leave?"

"Right. At least we know there's no way the twins can stay longer than a week—they *have* to go back to school." Steven raised his cup of tea. "Here's to next week—and our liberation from the Wakefield twins."

Billie raised her cappuccino. "I'll drink to that," she said with a smile.

Zach and Jessica drove up the coast to a cute little restaurant in the hills. The small bistro had hardwood floors and gingham curtains in the windows. A healthy fire crackled in a huge brick fireplace. Zach ordered a bottle of wine with dinner, and Jessica felt so sophisticated, sipping white wine along with her rabbit stew. She had never eaten rabbit, but Zach was right—it tasted a lot like chicken.

She looked across the table at Zach's sweet face. The flames of the fire reflected beautifully in his lustrous green eyes. The restaurant was perfect. Zach was perfect.

"I'm glad you suggested getting far away," Zach said, taking Jessica's hand and playing with her fingers. "This place is so warm and cozy. Even though it's not nearly cold enough to justify a fire, I like it."

Jessica looked at the fire. "Sometimes I wish I knew what a really cold winter felt like so I could appreciate the warmth of a fire," she mused.

"I thought you told me you lived in Boston until you were twelve," Zach said, looking confused. "Don't you remember the cold winters?"

"I mean, we didn't have a fireplace in my house," Jessica said quickly. "So tell me about the house you grew up in."

Zach described the two-family home where he'd lived as a child in upstate New York. "It was on a block where just about every house had a family with kids," he reminisced. "During the summer all the kids would play hide-and-seek, while the parents sat on their front porches drinking lemonade."

Jessica put her chin in her hands. "Sounds nice,"

she said, easily forming a picture in her mind. Zach was so expressive.

"It was," Zach said, smiling a bittersweet smile. "Then my father got transferred, and we had to move to Virginia." He grimaced.

"What's wrong with Virginia?" Jessica asked.

"Oh, nothing's wrong with Virginia, but—" He paused and stared into his water glass, deep in thought. "Well, I left all my friends back in New York, and when we moved, I had trouble feeling like I fit in." He looked at Jessica. "You moved to a different city when you were twelve, so you should know how hard it can be. Or maybe it wasn't hard for you—you're so confident."

"It *was* an adjustment," Jessica said noncommittally. She had to move the conversation back to him. "But I can't imagine why you would have trouble making friends. You're so easygoing and friendly."

"I think that was part of my problem. People in upstate New York were real and honest—everyone trusted each other. People in Virginia were different," he said, taking a bite of his filet of sole.

"In what way?"

Zach finished chewing. "All the kids' parents worked for the government, and they were always bragging about their parents, and I never knew whether they were telling the truth or exaggerating," Zach said glumly. "They even made me wonder if my father was really who he said he was. I mean, he said he worked for a big research company, but all the kids said I was naive. Supposedly, anyone in Washington who said he did research was actually a spy working for the CIA."

Jessica gasped. "Do you think he was really a spy?"

Zach tore off a chunk of bread and chomped down on it. "I could never figure it out."

"You never asked?" Jessica knew she would have confronted her father right away if someone had told her Ned Wakefield was a spy. Having a father who was a spy would be totally romantic, much better than having a boring old lawyer for a father.

"Sure, I asked," Zach continued. "Every time he went on a business trip, I would ask him all sorts of questions. And when he gave me vague answers, I just knew he was lying. I started not to trust my own father. I hated that." Zach looked down at his plate in silence. Jessica didn't know what to say.

Zach looked up at her. "Well, enough about my childish worries." He reached for his wine. "Here's to honesty," he said, raising the glass for a toast.

Jessica raised her glass to meet his. She took a big gulp of her wine, which didn't do anything to help the feeling of guilt growing inside her. Zach looked so hurt, so sad, when he talked about feeling as if his father had lied to him. *He would be devastated if he found out I've been lying to him, too,* she realized.

Elizabeth was on a roll, her fingers flying over the keyboard. Once she had decided to write about the problem of alcohol on campus, the ideas kept coming so fast, she could barely keep up.

For many students, freshman year is their first time away from home, away from the watchful eyes of their parents. With this new freedom comes both reward and risk: the reward of being able to assert one's independence is tempered by the risk of making huge mistakes. Unfortunately, too many young people at universities today make the very same mistake. Namely, they think that the best way to enjoy their newfound freedom is to spend every weekend drowning themselves in a bottle.

Elizabeth paused to read over the words she had just written. She backspaced to change the last words to: *drowning themselves in a beer bong.*

Elizabeth smiled. *Will Felicia Newkirk know what a beer bong is?* she wondered. Elizabeth herself hadn't known until Saturday night. Three guys in the kitchen had been piecing together a contraption made out of a funnel attached to a rubber tube. "It makes it easier to guzzle lots of beer faster," one of the guys had explained when she had asked what they were doing.

Many students have turned the activity of getting drunk into a science. One can only imagine how many wonderful new engineering innovations these young people might discover if they would put their minds to something more constructive than the search for the next buzz.

Even though Elizabeth had thought that she

didn't have enough experience to write an essay on college life, she soon realized that if she herself had been a college freshman, she wouldn't have been as comfortable writing this essay. *Journalists are supposed to be objective,* Elizabeth remembered. *Maybe this topic was actually the best I could have found.*

Elizabeth was so engrossed in her writing that she didn't even hear the front door open and close.

"Liz! Are you still up?" Jessica called from the living room.

Elizabeth almost jumped out of her seat. "I'm in here," she answered after she had regained her composure.

Jessica burst into the bedroom. "You'll never believe the restaurant Zach took me to. It was so romantic—the menu was all in French, and Zach bantered with the waiter in his own language. Foreign languages are just so sexy. Especially French!" Jessica bent to take off a shoe, but when she tried to balance on one foot, she stumbled into the room, almost knocking over the lamp on the nightstand. She reached for the bed to steady herself, but her hand just missed and she went tumbling to the floor. She broke into a fit of laughter.

Elizabeth narrowed her eyes. "Jess," she asked sternly. "Have you been drinking?"

Jessica stopped laughing and looked at her sister. Her cheeks were flushed. "We just had some wine with dinner," she explained. "It's no big deal."

"But Zach drove—"

"Yes, Zach drove," Jessica said huffily, getting up off the floor and onto the bed. "That's why *I'm* the one who got buzzed—he stopped drinking after one glass, and the waiter kept refilling mine. Give me a break, Liz, do you think I'm stupid? Do you think I'd get into a car with someone who was drunk?"

"No, I'm sorry. I think this essay is getting to me," Elizabeth said.

"Tell me about it. Zach would never do anything to endanger me," Jessica proclaimed. "He respects me."

Elizabeth looked at her sister. "But do you respect Zach?" she asked.

"What in the world do you mean by that?" Jessica demanded.

"I don't think it's very respectful to be lying to Zach about being in college," Elizabeth said.

"Oh, Liz, you're so literal," Jessica said, standing up. "You should have sat in on this philosophy class yesterday. Because it's just like the professor said: What is truth, really?" Elizabeth groaned, but that didn't stop Jessica. "Zach makes me feel more special than any guy I've ever met," she gushed. "He makes me feel like a woman." Jessica swooned against the door, her hands over her heart.

"What about Ken?" Elizabeth asked.

Jessica glared at her. "What about Ian?" she said sassily. She marched back into the living room.

"It's not the same thing at all!" Elizabeth called after her twin. "Ian and I are just friends."

Jessica grumbled something from the other room.

"What was that?" Elizabeth called.

"Oh, nothing," Jessica responded. "Just go back to your essay!"

Elizabeth rolled her eyes when she heard the TV click on. She sighed and turned back to the computer.

"Jessica!" Elizabeth called from the bedroom. "Would you mind turning the volume down? I'm trying to concentrate in here."

Groaning, Jessica reached her arm out to find the remote. It wasn't anywhere within reach. "It's just a commercial, Liz," she called to her twin. "The volume will go down when the show comes back on." At home Jessica rarely got the chance to watch late-night talk shows—her parents wouldn't let her. So she was taking advantage of the opportunity.

"*Now,* Jess," Elizabeth called again, her voice more insistent.

"OK, OK. Calm down." Jessica lifted her body off the couch to go in search of the remote. She found it next to the empty portable-phone unit. She almost jumped out of her skin when the phone rang in the other room.

"I've got the phone in here with me," Elizabeth called out. "Do you want me to answer?"

"No, I got it," Jessica said, scrambling to the kitchen to get the phone. She had a feeling it was Zach calling, and she didn't want to give Elizabeth an opportunity to expose her lie.

It *was* Zach. "I'm sorry to call you so late, but I just couldn't fall asleep until I asked you something."

"That's OK, Zach. What do you want to ask me?" Jessica twirled the phone cord around her finger.

"We're having a formal dinner at Zeta House on Saturday, and I was wondering if you would be my date."

"Of course!" Jessica responded immediately. "I would love to be your date."

"I wasn't even sure if I wanted to go, but now that I have a wonderful woman to bring with me, I wouldn't miss it," Zach told her.

"That's so sweet," Jessica cooed. "I had a wonderful time tonight."

"Me, too," Zach whispered hoarsely. He asked if he could see her the next evening after his classes. "When are you done with your classes tomorrow?" he asked.

"Oh, I finish early on Tuesdays," Jessica responded.

"Great! Why don't I pick you up at five?"

"Well—" Jessica stopped to think. She didn't want to deal with the complications of Zach meeting Steven. "Why don't we just meet somewhere?" she suggested.

Zach suggested a popular diner on the north side of campus. "But just because I'm seeing you tomorrow doesn't mean I'm letting you off the hook for the formal dinner," Zach said. "So don't even think about backing out."

"An earthquake wouldn't keep me away," Jessica answered. They murmured their good nights and Jessica hung up.

One second later the phone jangled again.

"Miss me already?" Jessica said in her sexiest voice.

"How'd you know it was me?" Ken asked.

Oops! Jessica gasped. She recovered quickly. "I could tell by the way the phone rang," she said sweetly.

"I do miss you," Ken said.

"Me, too," Jessica whispered, twisting the phone cord tightly around her finger.

Elizabeth took another sip from the mug and grimaced. Her coffee was now cold and bitter, but she forced herself to down it in gulps. She needed the caffeine.

Her essay was still not quite where she wanted it to be. The thoughts were all there, they just weren't organized into a compelling enough argument. It had to be airtight.

"Are you still working on your essay?" a voice whispered to her from the doorway. Elizabeth turned around to see Steven and Billie looking at her in amazement.

Elizabeth rubbed her burning eyes. "I'm not done yet."

"Well, you better get done, or finish it tomorrow," Steven said impatiently. "We need to go to bed, and Jessica's already snoring on the sofa bed."

"I can't finish it tomorrow—I have to have it on Felicia Newkirk's desk by nine o'clock sharp," Elizabeth said, hearing her voice whine.

"C'mon, Liz," Steven said, sounding more impatient. "It's nearly two in the morning. Billie and I have been moving from one place to the next all night. We went to the library, and to the Coffee House. Then we went for ice cream, and *then* we went to the lounge in one of the dorms and watched every late-night talk show known to mankind. Now we really, really want to go to sleep."

Elizabeth gave Steven her most woeful expression. "This essay is really important, Steven. In fact, my future in journalism is riding on it. If Felicia Newkirk thinks I'm talented, she could open so many doors for me. Please let me stay up and work," she begged. "You guys can go to sleep. The only light I need is from the screen."

Steven looked obstinate. But before he refused her, Billie spoke up. "Of course you can use the computer," she said. "We'd never forgive ourselves if we were the ones who stood in the way of your brilliant career, would we, Steven?"

Steven pouted.

"Would we, Steven?" Billie pressed.

Steven finally grunted his agreement.

"I'll be so quiet, you won't even know I'm here," Elizabeth said gratefully.

"Don't be silly," Billie said. "I can't let you

work in the dark—it's murder on your eyes. We'll just sack out in sleeping bags on the living-room floor."

Steven shook his head and looked up at the ceiling. "Another perfect end to another perfect day," he muttered.

Chapter 12

"Don't you have something to do today?" Elizabeth snapped, jolting Jessica out of the dream she'd been having about Zach.

"Good morning to you, too," Jessica murmured, pulling the comforter over her head.

"Is it morning? I wouldn't know—I stayed up all night in front of that damn computer," Elizabeth grumbled.

Jessica opened her eyes to see Steven and Billie rolling up their sleeping bags. "Why'd you guys sleep out here?"

"I don't want to talk about it," Steven said. Jessica didn't push the topic—she didn't really care. All she cared about was getting more sleep. *I'm not going to be robbed of my rightful sleep again this morning,* she decided, covering her head with a pillow in an attempt to block out the sounds of clanking dishes and blow dryers.

Finally everyone left. Determined to get more sleep, Jessica tossed and turned to get comfortable. But the memory of her conversation with Ken the night before kept her from relaxing. He had sounded so sweet, so trusting, telling her how much he missed her. Jessica felt like a lout for dating Zach.

But then she reminded herself about how mad she had been at Ken when he'd thought she had cheated on the SAT. *Zach would never doubt my intelligence,* Jessica realized. *He knows how smart I am, and on top of that, he really likes it.*

The phone jangled Jessica out of her thoughts. Jessica tried to shake off her sleepiness and picked up the receiver.

"Jess? It's Magda. Are you up?"

"Um, sure—I was just reading," Jessica answered groggily. *Oh no! She* did *see me out with Zach last night!*

"All the girls really liked you yesterday," Magda said. "So we thought it would be fun if you and your sister came to have lunch at the house today—if you're free." Jessica, who had been holding her breath, panted quietly for air.

"After all," Magda continued, "it's never too early to start rushing."

"I would love to come," Jessica said, sitting up to collect her thoughts. "I don't know how to get in touch with Elizabeth, though. She's already left for campus."

"Doesn't Elizabeth *want* to be a Theta?" Magda asked.

"Of course she does," Jessica answered quickly.

"Well, you just tell her if she doesn't start acting like a pledge, we'll have serious doubts about whether she's qualified to be a Theta," Magda warned.

"I will," Jessica responded. *I wonder how qualified Magda would think I was if she knew I was dating Zach.*

Jessica was in her element, sitting in the Theta House dining room with Darcy, Magda, and Amanda and a few new girls. The room was buzzing with talk and laughter.

"Does anyone want anything else?" Magda asked as she pushed her chair back from the dining-room table. "I'm going up for more of that yummy lasagna."

"Could you get me some juice?"

"I could use some more bread."

"Is there any frozen yogurt left?"

"Hold it!" Magda put her hand up to stop the requests. "Do I look like an octopus?"

"I'll help you," Jessica offered.

She followed Magda into the kitchen. "The lasagna is scrumptious today, Maria—not like last time," Magda said to the woman cutting vegetables behind the counter. "I'm glad you took my suggestion about using fresh tomatoes instead of the canned ones."

"Thank you, Ms. Helperin. I'm glad you like it,"

Maria said humbly. Jessica watched the exchange with interest. Lila had always had servants and cooks, but Jessica had never enjoyed that luxury. She found the prospect quite attractive.

"That's so cool that you have a cook," Jessica said after she and Magda returned to the table with the girls' requests.

"We don't think of Maria as our cook, she's like one of the girls," Darcy said. "We invite her to all our parties."

"Does she come?" Jessica asked, curious. The girls exchanged looks.

"I think she came to one," Darcy said tentatively.

"Oh, that's right!" Magda squealed. "Remember that greasy guy she brought along with her? The one with all the chest hair and the missing front tooth?" The girls broke into a fit of giggles. Jessica smiled, then stopped. Maria had just come out of the kitchen to replenish the Parmesan cheese. She caught Jessica's eye and looked down, hurrying back into the kitchen. The look on Maria's face made Jessica feel sick. *How would I feel if a bunch of privileged girls treated me as if I were their servant?* she asked herself. *And made fun of my boyfriend right in front of my face?*

"I'm surprised that Liz still hasn't come by," Amanda said suddenly, pushing thoughts of Maria out of Jessica's head.

"Oh, that sister of mine always has something going on," Jessica said lightly. "In fact, she was up all night working on an essay in a journalism contest. She'll probably win, too—she always succeeds at everything she puts her mind to." Even though journalism was pretty geeky, Jessica figured that if she made Elizabeth out to be an ambitious go-getter, the girls would forgive her lack of devotion to the Thetas.

"It's so easy to get blackballed," Amanda continued, oblivious to Jessica's last statement. "She doesn't want to ruin her chances so early in the game."

"This one girl I know was rushing Kappa, and she got blackballed just for wearing the same dress to a fraternity dinner that the sorority president was wearing," Magda added. Jessica felt a knot forming in her stomach.

Darcy jumped in. "I remember that story. But at least she got into another house. I heard about a girl who couldn't get into a single sorority—not even the pitiful Pi Beta Phi—just because someone found out she'd made out with two guys in one night."

"Two guys in one night? How vulgar," Magda said, her eyebrows raised in disgust.

"At the same time?" Jessica asked, her eyes wide.

"Oh, gross," Darcy screeched. "No, not at the same time. It was during rush week, and this girl spent the afternoon with her boyfriend from back home. Then later, after he left, she got drunk at a party and made out with someone there." Jessica nodded her understanding.

"Did you hear about that girl who got kicked out for dating one of her sorority sister's *ex*-boyfriends?"

another girl asked. Jessica barely listened as the girls relayed one horror story after another. The knot in her stomach stretched tighter with each account. *If Magda finds out about me and Zach, even the worst sorority on campus would reject me,* she realized.

After lunch the girls all sat in the TV room. A soap opera played in the background, but the girls were engrossed in a heated debate about which was sexier—microminis, or slinky long skirts.

"Well, we could sit here and fight about this all day," Magda said after Darcy brought up the issue of slits and pleats. "But Jessica doesn't have very much time to learn about college life. What do you want to do with your short time on campus?" she asked Jessica.

"We could take you to some classes," Darcy suggested. "My four o'clock anthropology class is pretty interesting—'Folklore from Antiquity to the Present.'"

"Or you could come with me to modern poetry," Amanda said. "There's this really sexy junior who's always reading his poems out loud."

"Sure, either one of those sounds fine," Jessica said breezily, stifling a yawn. The sexy poet sounded promising, but Jessica had enough guys to think about at the moment. Besides, she'd already sat in on a college class the day before with Zach. What more did she need to know?

Then Magda snapped her fingers. "I've got a better idea. Let's go shopping!"

Minutes later Jessica was in heaven. She was on her way to the mall in Amanda's forest-green Mazda Miata, with a pair of borrowed sunglasses on her face. At one point, when they were stopped at a light, the car next to them honked.

"Hey, girls! Where's the party this afternoon?" a couple of burly-looking guys called over to them. Jessica and Amanda just laughed. As soon as the light turned green, Amanda threw the car into gear, leaving the guys to eat their exhaust.

Jessica glanced at the clock on the dashboard. It was two in the afternoon. *If I were back in my regular life, I would be fighting to keep my eyes open in boring old American history right now. I'm definitely going to like college,* she decided, stretching her arms high above her head.

After almost falling asleep in Steven's legal-theory class, Elizabeth decided to skip going with him to History of the Middle East. She longed to go back to the apartment and take a nap, but she worried that if she surrendered to her fatigue, she'd never wake up in time for the evening journalism seminar.

Now she sat on one of the benches in the main quad, watching the bustle of students. Oddly, she didn't feel out of place sitting there by herself. She felt as if she fit right in. Elizabeth fantasized about actually being a freshman, going to classes, getting involved in activities, having intellectual conversations until the early-morning hours.

"Fancy meeting you here," a familiar voice said.

Elizabeth looked up to see Ian's smiling face. "Ian! How are you?" she asked. She hadn't minded being alone, but she was happy to see someone she knew.

"Besides being almost comatose? I stayed up until three A.M. writing that cursed essay," he said, collapsing onto the bench. He had dark circles under his eyes. "Did you end up writing anything, or did you blow it off?"

"I certainly did not blow it off," Elizabeth said huffily. "I even beat you—I didn't turn off the lights until five thirty."

"Are you serious?" Ian asked, taken aback. "You actually wrote an essay for old Felicia? Even after she put you through the wringer yesterday?"

"That's exactly why I had to write a great essay," Elizabeth said. "If I can get Felicia Newkirk to take me seriously, she could be really great for my career."

"You're really ambitious, aren't you?" Ian looked at her with respect.

"Ian, being a journalist is my dream—it's the only thing I've ever really wanted to do with my life," Elizabeth said earnestly.

Ian smiled. "I have to hand it to you. I don't think I was so driven when I was your age." Elizabeth looked at him crossly. "Not that I think you're young or anything," he added.

"Thank you," Elizabeth said. Then she let out an involuntary shiver, remembering her pitiful performance in class the day before. "I sure felt young yesterday, though. I can't remember ever feeling so humiliated. Your classmates must think I'm a complete idiot."

Ian chuckled. "Actually, since you brought it up, let me tell you something that will make you feel better," Ian said. "I bumped into one of the guys from class when I was dropping off my paper, and he asked me about you."

"What did he say?" Elizabeth asked, mortified. "What did you say?"

"Don't worry about it," Ian said with a smile. "He was just asking if you were single. He thought you were cute."

"He thought I was *cute*? After I came off looking like a *ditz*?" Elizabeth gasped in disbelief. "And you thought that would make me *feel* better?"

"I just—" Ian began.

"I can't *believe* it," Elizabeth railed. "I thought guys in college were different. I thought they would be interested in women who actually have brains in their heads."

"*I'm* interested in women with brains," Ian said. He took Elizabeth's hand.

Elizabeth gasped at his touch. She looked up to see Ian gazing deep into her eyes. His cheeks were flushed. She put her other hand over his. "Ian, I *told* you I have a boyfriend," she said gently.

"I know, I just thought—" He stopped and bit his lip.

Elizabeth squeezed his hand. "What?" she asked.

"Forget it," Ian said. He scooted away from her on the bench. "So what did you write about, anyway?" Ian asked. His voice sounded formal and distant, and the warmth Elizabeth had felt from him was gone. *I guess I was wrong,* she thought sadly. *Ian won't be satisfied just being my friend.*

"So how's your college romance?" Magda asked out of the blue. They were in the hottest clothing boutique in town, flipping through the sales racks.

"Oh, he turned out to be a dud," Jessica responded breezily.

"Too bad," Magda said.

After they finished collecting the things they wanted to try on, they headed for the fitting rooms.

"Oh, let's share," Magda said. "I always love having a second opinion, and these dressing rooms are really spacious."

"Sure," Jessica agreed.

They had gone through a couple outfits apiece when there was a knock on the door. "I found that dress you wanted in your size," a voice on the other side of the door said. "Do you still want to try it on?"

"Definitely," Magda said, opening the door wide.

Jessica was shocked to see the saleswoman holding an electric-blue silk gown. It was long and slinky, covered in fancy beadwork. Magda grabbed the dress and held it up to her body. The dramatic blue looked great against her fair complexion, jet-black hair, and crystal-blue eyes.

Jessica whistled. "What's that for?"

Magda smiled. "The Zeta formal dinner dance."

Jessica gulped. *This can't be happening,* she thought with a tinge of panic.

"My date's a real jerk," Magda continued. "But I know Zach Marsden is going to be there. And I plan to make my move. Heaven help anyone who tries to stand in my way!"

Jessica groaned inwardly. *Of course Magda's going to be at the dance,* she berated herself. *And it looks like I might be kissing my Theta membership good-bye.*

Chapter 13

"'Bye! Talk to you later!" Jessica shouted and waved as Amanda's Miata roared off. As she turned to walk up the stairs to Steven's apartment, her mind started whirling with confusion.

What am I going to do? she wondered. Jessica knew that if Magda found out she was dating Zach, she would be blacklisted for life. She would never get into Theta Alpha Theta, not at any university in the whole United States. And Magda would tell Zach she'd been lying to him. Zach would never speak to her again.

Then there was the issue of Ken. Jessica loved Ken. When she thought of losing him over this, after all their false stops and starts, she felt a stab of pain shoot all the way from her throbbing temples to her feet, which were already aching from an afternoon of shopping.

What am I going to do? she asked herself again. Then the solution came to her—the one she hadn't allowed herself to consider before. But she had no choice. *I should break up with Zach. Let Magda have him. That would solve all my problems.*

Except for the problem that she really liked Zach. There was something really special about him. When she was with him, she felt witty, bright, thoughtful, and knowledgeable. *He challenges me to be smart, and I like that feeling.* To top that off, Zach was extremely cute and looked great in his Levi's.

Jessica arrived at Steven's door and she burst into the apartment. "What am I going to do?" she asked herself once again, but this time it came out in a loud wail. She slammed the door behind her and flicked on the light. It wasn't until then that she noticed Billie lying on the couch.

Jessica gasped. "Oh, Billie, I'm sorry. I didn't know anyone was home." She saw that the curtains were drawn and jazz music played softly on the stereo.

Billie sat up, her hair rumpled. "It's OK," she said drowsily, rubbing her eyes. "I was just trying to catch up on some lost sleep." She looked at Jessica, taking in the distressed look on her face. "What are you going to do about what?" she asked.

"Oh, my life is a mess, that's all," Jessica said, throwing her purse onto the hall table. "Don't worry, there's nothing you can do about it. There's nothing anyone can do," she whimpered, letting her body collapse against the wall.

"Try me," Billie offered.

Jessica looked at Billie. She was burning to tell someone about her dilemma. She had already ruled out calling Lila. Knowing her best friend as well as she did, Jessica knew this story would be too juicy for Lila to keep to herself. She'd tell one friend, and that girl would tell two friends, and pretty soon everyone at Sweet Valley High would know that Jessica Wakefield was dating a premed student behind her future sorority sister's back. *I'd be humiliated,* Jessica thought. *Everyone would know my stupid situation. Including Ken.*

Jessica cringed at the thought of Ken hearing this story through the grapevine. No, Jessica couldn't turn to Lila.

And Elizabeth would offer no solace. She had already voiced her disapproval—many times—over Jessica's lying to Zach and dating someone behind Ken's back. If Jessica told her about the Magda complication, Elizabeth would be less than sympathetic.

But should she tell Billie? What if Billie told Steven that she was dating a college guy and lying about her age? Steven would surely tell their parents, who would hit the roof and demand that she return home immediately.

But she had to tell someone, or pretty soon she would explode. And anyway, Billie had already met

Zach, and she hadn't given Jessica a hard time about it yet.

"OK," Jessica said, sinking down on the couch next to Billie. "You asked for it. But you've got to promise not to tell anyone." Billie agreed to be discreet, so Jessica unloaded her story.

"But it's not like Magda is dating Zach," Billie reasoned after Jessica had explained the situation. "I mean, you didn't even know Magda when you met Zach."

"That doesn't matter," Jessica explained. "I should have backed down right away when I found out that Magda liked him."

"So why didn't you?" Billie looked at her earnestly.

"Because I didn't want to! I really like Zach!"

"But don't you already have a boyfriend anyway?" Billie asked, raising her eyebrows.

Jessica just looked at Billie and heaved a sigh. "You're not helping me at all, Billie!" She buried her face in her hands.

"Wait, wait. I'm sorry," Billie said. "I'm just trying to piece all the information together. So what was this about your lying to Zach about being in college?" Jessica explained how the lie to Zach had started honestly enough, until all of a sudden she realized she couldn't back down from her story without looking like a complete idiot.

"I still think you should tell everyone the truth," Billie said, her brown eyes serious. "It's the only way out. Otherwise you'll just keep digging your hole deeper and deeper."

"But don't you see? It's too late for truth! I've caused too much damage already," Jessica sobbed. "Maybe I should just leave. Escape to Antarctica, where no one will find me."

"I don't think it's ever too late for the truth," Billie added softly.

"Obviously, Billie, you just don't know how things work in the real world," Jessica said. Then she spotted the clock on the wall. It was ten to five! She was supposed to meet Zach for an early dinner at five on the north side of campus. How had it got so late?

"Oh, my gosh—I've got to get ready and get out of here." Jessica jumped up and ran to the bathroom, leaving Billie with her mouth hanging open.

Jessica had just finishing spritzing her bangs with hair spray when she heard a knock on the door.

"I'll get it," Billie yelled. Jessica rushed out of the hallway to see Zach standing in the hallway, looking at Billie in confusion.

Jessica gasped. "Zach! What are you doing here?"

Jessica quickly made up a reason why Billie was welcoming visitors to the apartment Jessica was supposed to be living in alone. And why she stayed behind after Jessica and Zach had left. "She was locked out of her room, so she needed a place to hang out for the afternoon until her roommate comes home from her job," Jessica explained.

She walked with Zach across campus to the diner. He was holding her hand possessively. At any other time Jessica would have been thrilled that her date was so open about public displays of affection. But now she was terrified of being discovered.

Zach was telling her a story about the first time he'd tried to get onto a surfboard. "There was this old guy out there—he must have been nearly seventy—and he was catching these ten-foot swells while I wasn't even managing to sit on my board for more than five minutes without falling off."

Jessica laughed absentmindedly. She was trying to listen to Zach, but her eyes were too busy darting around, keeping an eye out for Magda, or one of the Thetas, or anyone who knew Magda or one of the Thetas. Not to mention how annoying it would be to run into Elizabeth or Steven.

Jessica's nerves were shot. *I'm going to be the first person in the state of California who dies from a heart attack before her seventeenth birthday,* she thought.

Billie's words came back to her: *It's never too late for the truth.* Was Billie right? Maybe Jessica should just tell the truth, come clean, to everyone. Even she had to admit that sometimes she had got herself into real trouble by telling one lie after another.

She almost walked right past the diner, but Zach pulled on her arm to stop her. "Whoa," he said. "We're here."

They sat down in a roomy booth, and Jessica ordered a cheeseburger and a milk shake, hoping a meal would calm her nerves. But when the food came, she couldn't bear to touch it. She had absolutely no appetite.

Zach reached across the table and took her hand. "Is something wrong? You've been awfully quiet since I picked you up." He looked at Jessica with concern. "Are you mad that I barged in on you when we had agreed to meet here?" Zach had explained to Jessica that he'd been running late and knew he wouldn't have been able to make it all the way to the north side of campus by five o'clock. So he had taken a chance that she was running late, too.

"Because I know how some girls hate it when guys show up at their door early or unexpected. I promise, I'll never do it again," he said earnestly.

"No, I'm not upset about that. It was a nice surprise to have you come pick me up," she lied. It didn't help that he was so understanding and thoughtful. Jessica bit her lip. Her voice stuck in her throat. *Tell him. Now. Tell him everything,* she commanded herself.

She took a deep breath and opened her mouth to spill her guts. But when Jessica looked over at Zach's sweet, honest face, no words came out of her mouth. She looked down, focusing on the napkin she was twisting in her lap. *I can't do it. He'll hate me.*

"Jess, look at me, what's wrong? Have I done something?" Zach reached out a hand, lifting Jessica's chin to look into her eyes.

But when Jessica glanced up, she didn't see Zach. She saw Magda Helperin.

Jessica blinked, hoping that her frazzled mind was playing a cruel trick. But when she opened her eyes, she saw that it was no trick: Magda and a group of Thetas were standing just inside the front door of the restaurant, waiting to be seated.

Chapter 14

Elizabeth walked with Ian to the journalism building with a mixture of excitement and dread. There was one part of her that believed her essay was good, *really* good. Then there was this other nagging part of her that couldn't forget being totally humiliated the day before. And hearing the voice of Felicia Newkirk: *Well, at least you're pretty. . . . That's all a girl like you will need, anyway.*

Elizabeth slowed down her steps as a feeling of embarrassment washed all over her again. Suddenly she walked straight into Ian's outstretched hand. "Watch it, it's a red light," he said. Elizabeth looked up. They had come to the street that bordered campus. Across the street stood the Dwight School of Journalism. The building that had looked so warm and welcoming in the light of day looked dark and hostile in the twilight.

The light turned green and Ian nudged her forward. Trudging up the steps of the building, Elizabeth realized she couldn't take another attack of humiliation like the one she'd suffered the day before. Especially on only forty-five minutes of sleep.

The classroom buzzed with nervous energy. All the students had arrived early, everyone anxiously awaiting the announcement of the winner. Some students were speculating about what the winner would get.

"Do you think it's money?"

"Probably just extra credits."

"Maybe it's a cruise!" someone joked, and everyone laughed.

Elizabeth had been so focused on writing the essay to impress Felicia Newkirk that she had totally forgotten that the winner would get a prize. "What do *you* think the prize will be?" she asked Ian now.

Ian shrugged. "I've got no idea," he said brusquely. Elizabeth looked at Ian's sullen face. His long bangs hung over his glasses, hiding his eyes. Ever since he had tried to take her hand earlier, Elizabeth noticed that Ian hadn't once looked directly at her.

What seemed like the start of a great new friendship was turning into something much more complicated. Elizabeth had the distinct feeling that she made Ian uncomfortable. *Well, I'm not going to worry about that right now,* Elizabeth decided.

Just then Professor Newkirk walked in and cleared her throat. "Good evening, class. I'm glad to see you all made it." There were murmurs of greeting from the classroom.

Professor Newkirk put on her spectacles and glanced at the paper she'd put on her podium. Then she took off her glasses and stared off into space.

"Here comes a sermon," Ian mumbled under his breath. Elizabeth hoped not. The suspense was killing her.

But Ian was right. "Every journalist must strive for knowledge, truth, and objectivity," Professor Newkirk said imperiously. "The first two, although challenging, pose far less of a challenge than does the third: objectivity." Elizabeth understood what the professor was talking about, thinking back to the conversation she'd had in her head the night before.

"We in the field like to think of ourselves as completely objective. Yet sometimes even the best of us stumble." *What is she getting at?* Elizabeth wondered.

"It is when we are confronted with a discrepancy that we must call our judgment into question." Professor Newkirk paused, putting her glasses back on her face.

"Class, I must be the first to admit that I made a grave error in judgment yesterday." Elizabeth's heart started beating faster. "I called into question the ability of someone who then proceeded to vastly outperform every student in the class. Students, it is with apology and pride that I tell you the winner of the essay competition: Elizabeth Wakefield."

The whole room erupted.

"I can't believe it!"

"That's not fair!"

"But she's in high school!"

Hearing the students voice their surprise, Elizabeth couldn't help but feel that much more triumphant. *I knew I could do it, I just knew it,* she exulted. *I should never have doubted myself.*

Professor Newkirk cleared her throat and tapped her pen on the podium to get their attention. "If you have any doubts about my decision, you won't after you've heard a few lines of Ms. Wakefield's article." She adjusted her glasses to read from the paper on the podium.

"'For many students freshman year is their first time away from home, away from the watchful eyes of their parents,'" Professor Newkirk read. Elizabeth beamed. Hearing the world-famous journalist reading *her* words gave her goose bumps.

Professor Newkirk paused to look up at the students before continuing reading. "'One can only imagine how many wonderful new engineering innovations these young people might discover if they would put their minds into something more constructive than the search for the next buzz.'" Professor Newkirk took off her glasses, and the students shifted uncomfortably in their seats.

Then she announced the prize. Elizabeth's piece would be edited by Professor Newkirk and published in a national magazine. In addition, she had won a highly coveted internship with *The Chronicle,* the University's nationally distributed newspaper. And based on what she'd seen of Elizabeth's skills, Professor Newkirk thought the job would lead to a permanent position.

"Ms. Wakefield," Professor Newkirk intoned, "I suggest you take your high-school equivalency test, enroll in Sweet Valley University, and get on with the business of reporting!"

Ian patted Elizabeth on the back, and the other students murmured words of support. Elizabeth was speechless.

"Just one question, Ms. Wakefield," Professor Newkirk said suddenly. "What, exactly, is a beer bong?"

Steven looked out the window again, wondering where Elizabeth was. He had specifically told his sister that Billie was going to prepare a great dinner—chicken cacciatore, her specialty—and it wasn't like Elizabeth to be late without calling.

"But, then, nothing about Liz surprises me anymore," Steven said as he started setting the table. "Not after the last few days."

"Maybe we should start," Billie said. "I just took it off the stove, and I don't want the chicken to dry out."

Steven agreed, and they sat down to eat. Their dinner conversation was consumed with discussion of the twins' visit.

"The last four days have felt like four years," Billie said.

"Tell me about it," Steven agreed. "Soon, Billie, I promise, my sisters will be but a distant memory."

Billie laughed. "You'll never believe the situation Jessica's got herself into."

"What now?" Steven groaned.

Billie gasped. "Oh, wait. I promised not to tell."

Suddenly Elizabeth flew in the door, her face glowing. "Steven, Billie, how would you like to have me for a permanent apartment mate?" she gushed cheerfully.

Steven's fork clattered on his plate. Billie choked on her milk.

Elizabeth smiled at them both. "I won't be going back to Sweet Valley High," she announced. "I'm staying right here!"

Don't miss Sweet Valley High #119: **Jessica's Older Guy,** *the conclusion of this special three-part miniseries about Jessica and Elizabeth's college fling at Sweet Valley University!*

SIGN UP FOR THE SWEET VALLEY HIGH® FAN CLUB!

Hey, girls! Get all the gossip on Sweet Valley High's® most popular teenagers when you join our fantastic Fan Club! As a member, you'll get all of this really cool stuff:

- Membership Card with your own personal Fan Club ID number
- A Sweet Valley High® Secret Treasure Box
- Sweet Valley High® Stationery
- Official Fan Club Pencil (for secret note writing!)
- Three Bookmarks
- A "Members Only" Door Hanger
- Two Skeins of J. & P. Coats® Embroidery Floss with flower barrette instruction leaflet
- Two editions of *The Oracle* newsletter
- Plus exclusive Sweet Valley High® product offers, special savings, contests, and much more!

Be the first to find out what Jessica & Elizabeth Wakefield are up to by joining the Sweet Valley High® Fan Club for the one-year membership fee of only $6.25 each for U.S. residents, $8.25 for Canadian residents (U.S. currency). Includes shipping & handling.

Send a check or money order (do not send cash) made payable to "Sweet Valley High® Fan Club" along with this form to:

SWEET VALLEY HIGH® FAN CLUB, BOX 3919-B, SCHAUMBURG, IL 60168-3919

NAME ______________________________
(Please print clearly)

ADDRESS ______________________________

CITY ____________________ STATE ________ ZIP ____________
(Required)

AGE ____________ BIRTHDAY ________ / ________ / ________

Offer good while supplies last. Allow 6-8 weeks after check clearance for delivery. Addresses without ZIP codes cannot be honored. Offer good in USA & Canada only. Void where prohibited by law.

LCI-1383-123

Bantam Books in the Sweet Valley High series
Ask your bookseller for the books you have missed

#1 DOUBLE LOVE
#2 SECRETS
#3 PLAYING WITH FIRE
#4 POWER PLAY
#5 ALL NIGHT LONG
#6 DANGEROUS LOVE
#7 DEAR SISTER
#8 HEARTBREAKER
#9 RACING HEARTS
#10 WRONG KIND OF GIRL
#11 TOO GOOD TO BE TRUE
#12 WHEN LOVE DIES
#13 KIDNAPPED!
#14 DECEPTIONS
#15 PROMISES
#16 RAGS TO RICHES
#17 LOVE LETTERS
#18 HEAD OVER HEELS
#19 SHOWDOWN
#20 CRASH LANDING!
#21 RUNAWAY
#22 TOO MUCH IN LOVE
#23 SAY GOODBYE
#24 MEMORIES
#25 NOWHERE TO RUN
#26 HOSTAGE
#27 LOVESTRUCK
#28 ALONE IN THE CROWD
#29 BITTER RIVALS
#30 JEALOUS LIES
#31 TAKING SIDES
#32 THE NEW JESSICA
#33 STARTING OVER
#34 FORBIDDEN LOVE
#35 OUT OF CONTROL
#36 LAST CHANCE
#37 RUMORS
#38 LEAVING HOME
#39 SECRET ADMIRER
#40 ON THE EDGE
#41 OUTCAST
#42 CAUGHT IN THE MIDDLE
#43 HARD CHOICES
#44 PRETENSES
#45 FAMILY SECRETS
#46 DECISIONS
#47 TROUBLEMAKER
#48 SLAM BOOK FEVER
#49 PLAYING FOR KEEPS
#50 OUT OF REACH
#51 AGAINST THE ODDS
#52 WHITE LIES
#53 SECOND CHANCE
#54 TWO-BOY WEEKEND
#55 PERFECT SHOT
#56 LOST AT SEA
#57 TEACHER CRUSH
#58 BROKENHEARTED
#59 IN LOVE AGAIN
#60 THAT FATAL NIGHT
#61 BOY TROUBLE
#62 WHO'S WHO?
#63 THE NEW ELIZABETH
#64 THE GHOST OF TRICIA MARTIN
#65 TROUBLE AT HOME
#66 WHO'S TO BLAME?
#67 THE PARENT PLOT
#68 THE LOVE BET
#69 FRIEND AGAINST FRIEND
#70 MS. QUARTERBACK
#71 STARRING JESSICA!
#72 ROCK STAR'S GIRL
#73 REGINA'S LEGACY
#74 THE PERFECT GIRL
#75 AMY'S TRUE LOVE
#76 MISS TEEN SWEET VALLEY
#77 CHEATING TO WIN
#78 THE DATING GAME
#79 THE LONG-LOST BROTHER
#80 THE GIRL THEY BOTH LOVED
#81 ROSA'S LIE

#82 KIDNAPPED BY THE CULT!
#83 STEVEN'S BRIDE
#84 THE STOLEN DIARY
#85 SOAP STAR
#86 JESSICA AGAINST BRUCE
#87 MY BEST FRIEND'S BOYFRIEND
#88 LOVE LETTERS FOR SALE
#89 ELIZABETH BETRAYED
#90 DON'T GO HOME WITH JOHN
#91 IN LOVE WITH A PRINCE
#92 SHE'S NOT WHAT SHE SEEMS
#93 STEPSISTERS
#94 ARE WE IN LOVE?
#95 THE MORNING AFTER
#96 THE ARREST
#97 THE VERDICT
#98 THE WEDDING
#99 BEWARE THE BABY-SITTER
#100 THE EVIL TWIN (MAGNA)
#101 THE BOYFRIEND WAR
#102 ALMOST MARRIED
#103 OPERATION LOVE MATCH
#104 LOVE AND DEATH IN LONDON
#105 A DATE WITH A WEREWOLF
#106 BEWARE THE WOLFMAN (SUPER THRILLER)
#107 JESSICA'S SECRET LOVE
#108 LEFT AT THE ALTAR
#109 DOUBLE-CROSSED
#110 DEATH THREAT
#111 A DEADLY CHRISTMAS (SUPER THRILLER)
#112 JESSICA QUITS THE SQUAD
#113 THE POM-POM WARS
#114 "V" FOR VICTORY
#115 THE TREASURE OF DEATH VALLEY
#116 NIGHTMARE IN DEATH VALLEY
#117 JESSICA THE GENIUS
#118 COLLEGE WEEKEND

SUPER EDITIONS:

PERFECT SUMMER
SPECIAL CHRISTMAS
SPRING BREAK
MALIBU SUMMER
WINTER CARNIVAL
SPRING FEVER

SUPER THRILLERS:

DOUBLE JEOPARDY
ON THE RUN
NO PLACE TO HIDE
DEADLY SUMMER
MURDER ON THE LINE
BEWARE THE WOLFMAN
A DEADLY CHRISTMAS
MURDER IN PARADISE
A STRANGER IN THE HOUSE
A KILLER ON BOARD

SUPER STARS:

LILA'S STORY
BRUCE'S STORY
ENID'S STORY
OLIVIA'S STORY
TODD'S STORY

MAGNA EDITIONS:

THE WAKEFIELDS OF SWEET VALLEY
THE WAKEFIELD LEGACY: THE UNTOLD STORY
A NIGHT TO REMEMBER
THE EVIL TWIN
ELIZABETH'S SECRET DIARY
JESSICA'S SECRET DIARY